Santa Paws
Saves the Day

by Kris Edwards

SCHOLASTIC INC.

New York   Toronto   London   Auckland   Sydney
Mexico City   New Delhi   Hong Kong   Buenos Aires

For all my patrol buddies,
especially night team!

ISBN 0-439-57354-8

Cover illustration by Robert Hunt
Designed by Timothy Hall

12 11 10 9 8 7 6   7 8 9/0

Printed in the U.S.A.   40

First printing, November 2004

1

The dog had been lying under the kitchen table, keeping a very close eye out for any food scraps that might fall to the floor. It was extremely hard work, making sure that not one crumb ever lay around for more than a second or two, but he didn't mind. It was one of his contributions to the Callahan household.

So far that day he had tidied up after the family's breakfast (one Cheerio, a piece of burnt bacon, and a blob of blueberry jam), Mr. Callahan's lunch (a scrap of salami, two tiny pieces of cheese), and a midafternoon snack of toaster pizza (Gregory had peeled off a string of cheese and given it to him) and apples (Patricia had given him the core — one of his favorite treats — when she was done munching).

Kitchen-floor duty was especially good when the whole family was home all day. Usually, Santa Paws could count only on Mr. Callahan's lunch, since Tom was a writer who worked at

1

home on his computer. But this week Gregory and Patricia were on Christmas vacation, which meant that they didn't have to leave first thing every morning and stay away for most of the day, like they usually did. And their mother, Eileen Callahan, who taught physics at Ocean-port High School, stayed at home, too. Yay! It was *great* to have the whole family around all day long. Even Abigail and Evelyn, the Calla-hans' cats, seemed happiest when everyone was home.

But now Eileen was picking up her car keys from the kitchen table. That meant she was go-ing somewhere! Would he get to go, too? The dog leapt to his feet. He *loved* going places! Riding in the car was the *best*! He could watch out the window and see all kinds of interesting things. Plus, maybe there would be Milk-Bones where they were going. You never knew when some-body might give you a Milk-Bone.

Like, sometimes Mr. Callahan would invite the dog to ride along as he drove downtown to do er-rands. When they went to the bank, Tom would pull up next to a window thing, and the nice lady behind the glass would smile at the dog in the backseat. She would take the papers Tom gave her and, in return, give Tom a Milk-Bone. The dog *loved* helping Tom go to the bank.

The dog had been a little bit worried when the

new puppy joined their household, almost a year ago. Would he have to share his Milk-Bones with her? As it turned out, he loved her so much that he would have been happy to — but amazingly, she did not care one bit about Milk-Bones.

"Gregory! Patricia!" called Mrs. Callahan. "Time to head for the hospital!" She smiled down at the dog. "Santa Paws, where's Cookie? I know she'll want to come, too."

Cookie. Santa Paws's ears perked up at the name, and he cocked his head toward the kitchen door. Sure enough, along with the pounding footsteps of Patricia and Gregory coming down the stairs, he heard the dainty *click-click* of his best friend's toenails. Cookie must have been up in Patricia's room, napping in her favorite spot on the cushy purple velvet butterfly chair.

The dog raced to the door to greet the new arrivals. It seemed as if he hadn't seen Gregory and Patricia in *ages!*

"Hey, Santa Paws!" said Gregory, reaching down to give the dog's ears a rub. "What's up, big guy?" Even though Santa Paws was a large dog, weighing in at almost ninety pounds, the boy was tall for his age, so Gregory had to bend over pretty far. Sometimes, when he was really excited to see Gregory, Santa Paws helped by sitting up on his back legs and putting his paws on the boy's chest. The big dog and the boy

3

would dance and wrestle for a while until Mrs. Callahan begged them to settle down before they broke another lamp.

"Coming to the hospital with us, sweet pea?" asked Patricia, squatting down to kiss the dog on his nose. Even though she was seventeen, a year older than Gregory, she was smaller than her brother. Still, sometimes people mistook them for twins: the color of Patricia's ponytail matched Gregory's brown wavy hair exactly, and their eyes were the same bright blue.

Cookie bounced into the room, eyes shining and ears high. Seeing Santa Paws, she bounced even higher, then stretched out her front legs and gave him a devilish glance as she bowed, tail in the air and chest to the floor, in an invitation to play. "Chase me!" her look said.

Santa Paws bowed back, but didn't take her up on the idea of a game. He'd heard the word "hospital," and he knew there was no time for one of their wild chases around the house. They had work to do.

Santa Paws *loved* it when there was work to do.

Cookie? Not so much. But she was young, and she was learning.

Mrs. Callahan checked the collars on both dogs to make sure their yellow THERAPY DOG tags were showing. Then Santa Paws and Cookie followed Eileen, Gregory, and Patricia out to the car.

"Jump in," Patricia told Cookie. Patricia had been teaching Cookie all sorts of tricks in the last few months. Jumping was one of Cookie's favorites. She bounded into the backseat. Santa Paws, who had never understood the point of "tricks," didn't have to be told. He jumped in, too.

"My turn to drive!" Gregory said, as he slid behind the wheel. He was sixteen now, so Patricia wasn't the only Callahan teen with a license.

"Whatever," sighed Patricia, climbing into the backseat. "Just remember to take off the emergency brake, okay? And don't forget to signal when you're turning." At seventeen, she'd been driving for a year already and thought she knew it all.

"Thank you very much, Ms. Driver's Ed," Gregory said. "May I remind you that I've never run a stop sign?" he added with a wicked grin. "Unlike some people."

Patricia's face flushed bright red as she remembered the time last year when she'd rolled past the stop sign at the quiet intersection of Maple Lane and Chestnut Street, not quite coming to a complete stop. Her mistake had been spotted by, of all the policemen in Oceanport, her uncle Steve. Instead of a ticket, Uncle Steve had given her a stern warning. From then on, she had always stopped for at least a full five seconds at every red sign she saw.

After a little tussle over who would get to sit near the window (Santa Paws let Cookie win this time), Santa Paws and Cookie settled into the backseat next to Patricia. The big dog gazed lovingly at his family as Gregory backed the car out of the driveway. How could he have been so lucky, all those years ago, to be found and adopted by the most wonderful people in the world? He thought back to his days as a stray, a tiny puppy struggling to survive in a big, scary world. Hungry, cold, and miserable, he had wandered the streets of Oceanport looking longingly at the lucky dogs who rode in cars or walked next to their proud owners on leashes. His life had changed when he met Gregory — only ten years old then! — in the schoolyard. And on Christmas Day, soon after that meeting, Santa Paws had become part of the Callahan family.

Did Cookie know how lucky she was, too? Santa Paws glanced at her, taking in her tightly curled black coat, her alert expression, her big, bright brown eyes. Even sitting still, she looked as if she were bouncing. She was almost full-grown now, though not nearly as big as Santa Paws. But a year ago, when she had turned up looking for a home, she had been only a puppy herself, a little fluffy black thing.

6

Santa Paws had heard his family explaining about their dogs. "Santa Paws is part German shepherd and part collie," Mr. Callahan would say. "As for Cookie, who knows? We think her mom might have been an Airedale, because she has that curly coat and that scrappy terrier personality. And maybe her dad was a black Lab — that would would explain her coloring and her mania for chasing balls."

Santa Paws wasn't really sure what any of that meant. But he did know that Cookie was special. She drove him crazy sometimes, with her wild energy and her mischievous ways, but he tolerated all of that — and even joined in most of the time. Anyway, he knew Cookie would learn soon enough that life was not all fun and games.

A few minutes later, Gregory carefully pulled the car into a spot in the busy hospital parking lot and turned off the engine. "Everybody ready?" he asked.

Patricia clipped leashes onto both dogs, then handed the worn brown braided leather one to Gregory. "You take Santa Paws," she said. She picked up the neon pink-and-purple lead that was attached to the other dog. "Cookie's lead matches my outfit better," she explained, slipping her purple-framed sunglasses up on top of her head.

"This isn't a fashion show," Mrs. Callahan reminded Patricia, rolling her eyes at her daughter.

"Style always counts," said Patricia, as she climbed out of the car. "Right, Cookie?"

Cookie jumped out after Patricia, then pranced around joyously for a moment. Santa Paws stood calmly next to Gregory, watching the black dog's antics. Cookie was always happy, always eager to find out what fun thing would happen next.

When the Callahans and the two dogs walked into the Pediatrics Ward of Oceanport Memorial Hospital, they were greeted by the off-key but delightful sound of a group of small children singing "Deck the Halls." A dark-haired woman in a long denim jumper was waving her arms, directing the singers.

"Oh!" said Mrs. Callahan. "I can't believe I forgot Miranda's class was going to be here today." She peered at the group of children, who were clustered near the ward's Christmas tree, each wearing a red Santa hat. "There she is!" she cried, waving to her niece. Miranda was the older daughter of Tom Callahan's brother, Steve, and his wife, Emily. She'd be turning six soon; her little sister, Lucy, was almost three. Lucy and Miranda were the darlings of the extended Callahan clan.

Gregory gave Miranda a thumbs-up. In return, she gave him a gap-toothed grin, and he saw that she'd lost her second front tooth that week. Her Santa hat slipped down over one eye.

Patricia smiled at her. "You sound great," she mouthed.

Santa Paws waved his tail back and forth, happy as always to see his young friend.

But when Cookie spotted Miranda, a tail-wag just wasn't enough.

"Whoa! Cookie!" Patricia shouted, as the wire-haired black dog dashed forward, pulling her human companion off balance. Cookie hurtled straight into Miranda's arms.

"Fa, la, la, la — COOKIE!" shouted Miranda, interrupting her song. She threw her arms around her favorite friend. "Oh, I'm so glad you're here," she said, nuzzling Cookie's cheek with her own. "Cookie, Cookie, Cookie. Give me a kiss, Cookie!"

Cookie obeyed, instantly and happily, licking Miranda's cheek.

Santa Paws stood silently, watching. Gregory looked down at him. "You don't really approve, do you?" he asked his dog. "You think all dogs should be as mature and responsible as you are. Well, I could remind you of a few things *you* did when you were a puppy — or even last week!"

Santa Paws looked up at Gregory and wagged his tail.

Miranda's classmates — as well as a few patients who were able to leave their beds — clustered around Miranda and Cookie. After a few tries at keeping the song going, the chorus leader gave up trying to get them to finish "Deck the Halls." She was standing nearby with a bemused look on her face.

"Is that your dog?" A small boy with tousled blond hair approached Miranda. He wore a hospital gown and he was trailing a rolling IV stand with a bag of medicine that was hooked into his arm.

"Well . . ." said Miranda. "She lives with my cousins." She looked a little sad to have to admit this. Then she smiled. "But I named her!" She looked around at her growing audience. "Last Christmas, when she was just a little tiny puppy that my cousins adopted, she was at my house," she explained. "My mommy made two big batches of Christmas cookies. Like gingerbread men and trees and angels, all decorated with icing and rainbow sprinkles and everything."

"Yum," said a little girl with red braids and a cast on her right arm.

"They *were* yummy," Miranda said. "I ate three angels and one tree. And Lucy — that's my little sister — had a gingerbread man. I think Daddy had four. But guess who ate *all the rest!*" She pointed at Cookie. There were shrieks and groans from the audience.

"*All* of them?" asked the chorus director.

"All of them," Miranda said solemnly. She looked into Cookie's eyes and shook her head.

10

"And that's how she got her name!" She frowned. "But Mommy was not happy."

Cookie chose that moment to lean in and kiss Miranda again. Miranda giggled. "Sit pretty," she said to Cookie. The black dog jumped back and sat up eagerly, holding up her front paws.

"Are you begging?" asked Miranda with a giggle. "Cookie wants a cookie?"

Cookie jumped up again and stood wagging her tail so hard that her whole body wiggled.

Miranda shrugged. "Sorry," she said, holding up two empty hands. "No cookies today."

Cookie stopped wagging. She lay down and put her head between her front paws, looking dejected. But within a second, she was bouncing again. Cookie never stayed sad long.

"Nutter Butters are her favorite," Miranda told the other children. "But she also likes oatmeal-raisin and Fig Newtons."

"You mean she gets real cookies?" asked the red-haired girl. "I thought you meant, like, dog biscuits."

"Cookie won't eat dog biscuits," explained Miranda. "She only eats people cookies. Anything but chocolate chip. Chocolate isn't good for dogs, right, Cookie?"

Cookie sat up again, but this time she leaned forward to put her paws, gently, on Miranda's shoulders. She kissed her once again.

"Okay, Cookie," Patricia said. "That's enough

showing off. Let's let Miranda and her friends sing another song. Wave bye-bye!"

Obediently, Cookie lifted a paw and waved at the enthralled group of children.

"Good dog," said Patricia. "Now, take a bow!"

Once again, Cookie obliged, bowing deeply to her audience — the same way she'd bowed to invite Santa Paws to play. The children broke out in applause.

"Now, find Santa Paws!"

Cookie looked around until she spotted her friend, who was sitting patiently, waiting for her to remember his existence. She bounded over to join Santa Paws, Gregory, and Eileen Callahan, pulling Patricia behind her.

Santa Paws wagged his tail as his friend returned. He and Cookie touched noses.

"What a ham," said Gregory. "She always has to be the center of attention. You never should have taught her all those tricks."

"She's just a natural star," Patricia said, reaching down to ruffle Cookie's ears. "And the kids loved her."

Gregory couldn't argue with that. Cookie was always a crowd-pleaser, wherever she went. "Kids love Santa Paws, too," he couldn't help pointing out.

"Of course they do!" said Mrs. Callahan quickly, trying to head off a squabble. She hated it when Gregory and Patricia argued. "It's not a contest. But, speaking of kids, don't you think it's time to do our rounds? There are bedridden children who would love a visit from these two."

By then, Miranda and the other children had begun singing again. "Jingle bells, jingle bells, jingle all the way," they chorused happily.

The Callahans and their dogs went from room to room, visiting the children who couldn't get out of bed. It was always hard to see kids who were so sick: the ones who had no hair because they were having chemotherapy, the ones who seemed to be in pain, the ones who might never walk again. But Santa Paws knew just how to approach each child, and he always managed to leave even the sickest ones feeling just a bit better. Cookie was learning, too.

In the last room they visited, one bed was empty. In the other lay a little girl, about nine years old. Her mother sat near the head of the bed, smoothing the girl's hair back. "Look, Darlene," she said. "You have visitors!"

Darlene's eyes moved. She saw the dogs and the people. But she didn't smile or sit up.

Santa Paws knew what to do. He approached the side of Darlene's bed and lay his head near her shoulder. Patiently, he waited for her to reach out and stroke him.

She didn't move.

Darlene's mother sighed. "She usually *loves* dogs," she said. "But ever since we found out

13

Darlene has diabetes, she's been very sad. She hasn't even smiled for days. We miss our happy girl."

Santa Paws cocked an eyebrow and snuggled his head up a little closer. Was the girl going to pat him? He could wait all day if that's what it took.

"I have a friend with diabetes," Patricia told Darlene. "It was hard when she first found out — when she was about your age. But now she does all the same things I do, and her diabetes doesn't hold her back at all."

Darlene's mom smiled at Patricia gratefully. But Darlene frowned. "I bet she still has to give herself shots every single day," she said.

Patricia had to nod. "Yup," she admitted. "But she says she's used to it, and that it's not so bad."

"That's what everybody says," Darlene said. "But I *hate* shots more than anything."

"So does Cookie," said Patricia.

"Who's Cookie?" asked Darlene.

Patricia let Cookie approach Darlene's bed. "This is Cookie," she said. "Cookie," she asked. "Want to go to the vet and get a shot?"

Instantly, Cookie dropped to the floor to play dead. This was a trick she and Patricia had been working on. Cookie thought it was loads of fun — especially because everybody always laughed when she did it.

And Darlene was no exception. She couldn't

14

help herself. She looked down at Cookie and smiled. Then she broke into a giggle. When Cookie jumped to her feet and took a bow, Darlene laughed out loud. Then the girl rolled over and gave Santa Paws a big kiss on the nose.

After ten more minutes of showing off her best tricks, Cookie led the way out of Darlene's room, leaving a smiling girl and a grateful mom behind. Her eager prance made it clear that she felt her work was done. It was time to go home for a well-deserved cookie. And Santa Paws knew there was a Milk-Bone in his future, too.

2

"You should have seen her, Dad!" said Patricia, back at home. "Cookie is already a pro. She had that little girl laughing in no time." Patricia rummaged around in the cupboard next to the sink. "Ah, here we go," she said, pulling out a box of gingersnaps. "Ready for your treat, Cookie?"

Cookie didn't wait to be asked to sit. She knew the routine by now. She sat down right in front of Patricia and held up her paw for a shake.

Patricia laughed. "You're too much, Cookie," she said. "Every time I give you a treat, I make you sit and shake first. Now you're not even waiting for the commands!" She put her hands on her hips. "Time to teach you a new trick. How about a high five?" She held up her hand, down near Cookie's outstretched paw. "High five," she said, as she patted the dog's paw. "Good girl!" She gave Cookie a gingersnap and straightened up. "She'll learn that one in no time," she said. "Cookie is one smart cookie."

"Santa Paws is smarter," said Gregory, pulling out the box of Milk-Bones. "He's too smart to waste his time on silly tricks. Right, big guy?" He tossed a biscuit to Santa Paws, who snapped it out of the air. "Good catch."

The dog looked lovingly at Gregory as he chewed his treat. The afternoon at the hospital had been fun, but being home was even better. He'd had a Milk-Bone — yum! — and soon it would be time for dinner. In between, he could do anything he wanted. Like take a nap! What a great idea! Santa Paws thought for a moment. Should he nap in the living room, on the soft dog bed in the corner? Or should he go up to Gregory's room? There was a rug next to Gregory's bed, and he liked to bunch it up, scritching and scratching it into a comfy nest as he circled three or four times before settling down with a sigh.

"When's Uncle Steve coming over?" Patricia asked.

"He and Emily and the girls will be here for dinner," her mom answered. "They're bringing pizza from BonGiorno's."

"Sounds great," said Gregory. "I'll be in my room." He headed out of the kitchen, munching on a handful of gingersnaps.

That made the decision easy for Santa Paws.

If Gregory was going upstairs, he was going, too.

Cookie stayed behind in the kitchen, hoping for another cookie. But Patricia and her mom started to talk about a movie they'd watched the other night, and Mr. Callahan seemed completely absorbed in the newspaper. Bored, Cookie wandered off to lie down in the living room.

The Callahan house was quiet.

Upstairs, Santa Paws snored softly as he lay on the rug next to Gregory's bed. Gregory lay on the bed, one hand resting on Santa Paws's head, listening to a new CD on his Discman and singing along in a toneless mumble. Patricia headed for the computer to check her e-mail and IM her friends. Abigail and Evelyn, the Callahans' cats, were snoozing on the couch in the living room. And Tom and Eileen Callahan sat quietly together in the kitchen, reading the paper.

Then a car door slammed outside.

Santa Paws leapt to his feet, barking.

Downstairs, Cookie joined in, her bark a little higher-pitched.

Abigail and Evelyn stretched and yawned before they headed for the kitchen to see what was happening.

There was a knock at the back door.

Before Mr. Callahan could even say, "Come in," his brother, Steve, pushed the door open.

"Dinnertime!" he declared, holding out two boxes of pizza.

Emily and the two girls followed him in. "Where's Cookie?" demanded Miranda.

Cookie answered that question herself, skidding into the kitchen at a full gallop and hurling herself at Miranda. Dog and girl tumbled to the floor in a flurry of kisses and giggles.

Moments later, Santa Paws, Gregory, and Patricia arrived in the kitchen.

"I smell pepperoni," said Gregory, making a beeline for the boxes.

His uncle Steve smiled. "Hello to you, too," he said.

Patricia went over to give her uncle and aunt hugs. Then she scooped Lucy up into her arms. "How's my Lucy-loo?" she sang.

Santa Paws headed straight for Steve Callahan. The dog knew that this man was someone special in his life. Steve had been the first of the Callahans to see Santa Paws, all those years ago when the dog was a frightened stray. The young policeman had thought right away that this puppy might be the perfect addition to his brother's family, and he had done his best to bring them together. Now, in the kitchen, Santa Paws sat quietly next to Steve, leaning against his legs and looking up at him with serious brown eyes.

Mr. and Mrs. Callahan bustled around putting plates and a big bowl of salad on the table while Gregory helped himself to a slice of pizza from one of the boxes.

"Gregory, can't you wait?" asked his mother.

He shook his head, munching a mouthful. "Shtarving," he mumbled, around the cheese.

"Okay," said Mr. Callahan. "Let's eat!"

Santa Paws and Cookie took up their posts under the table, Santa Paws near Gregory's chair and Cookie near Miranda's. For a while, there wasn't much talking as everyone dug in to the steaming pizza.

Finally, Steve pushed his chair back. "I don't know," he said. "I used to be able to finish a pie by myself, but these days four slices seem to hold me." He patted his stomach.

"Right," Emily said drily. "You eat like a bird."

"Can Santa Paws have my pizza bones?" Gregory asked, holding up some leftover crusts.

"I think he's counting on it," said Mr. Callahan, nodding at Santa Paws. The dog was drooling slightly as he gazed up at Gregory. Leftover pizza crusts were one of his favorite treats. Cookie, who turned up her nose at them, didn't know what she was missing.

"So," said Steve. "Everybody excited about Christmas?"

"I am! I am!" chorused Miranda and Lucy.

Patricia smiled. "Sure," she said, with a little

shrug. She and Gregory were way past the age where Christmas made them wild with excitement, but it was still a favorite time of year.

"It'll be so great to be in Vermont again!" Steve said.

"You're going to Vermont for Christmas?" asked Gregory.

Steve shot Tom a look. "Oops," he said. "Guess you haven't told them yet."

"Told us what?" Patricia sounded suspicious.

"We were going to tell you tonight," her father explained. "We're all going to Vermont for Christmas. We were kind of keeping it as a surprise."

"Well — it worked," said Patricia. "I'm surprised."

"So am I," said Gregory, frowning. "What do you mean, we're all going to Vermont? Don't we get any say in the matter?"

Under the table, Santa Paws stirred. He had finished his pizza crusts, and now he was listening intently to the sound of the voices above him. Something wasn't quite right. Gregory did not seem happy.

"Let Dad explain," said Mrs. Callahan quickly. "Once you hear the plan, you'll love it."

"What if I have my *own* plans?" Gregory began. "I mean, my friends and I — "

"Yeah," Patricia interrupted. "It's not like we're little kids you can just drag around wherever you want anymore."

"Hey!" said Miranda.

"Sorry," said Patricia. "Didn't meant to insult little kids."

Mr. Callahan held up his hands. "Just hear me out," he said. "Mom's right. You'll love this idea. Gregory, you've been wanting to do more snowboarding, right? And Patricia, you always say that skiing once or twice a year isn't enough. Well, we're going to North Woods! All of us. For a whole week."

North Woods was a small ski area near Montpelier, the capital of Vermont. The Callahan grandparents lived in Montpelier, and Patricia and Gregory had skied at North Woods a few times when they had been visiting. They'd always had fun there.

"Are we staying with Granddad and Grammy?" Patricia asked.

Mr. Callahan shook his head. "They don't have room for all of us. So they've rented out an entire bed-and-breakfast, just for us! It's their Christmas present."

"And the best part," said Steve, "is that the B and B is right at North Woods. You can ski out the door and down to lift Three!"

Gregory remembered that lift Three was the chairlift that serviced the terrain park, where all the snowboarders hung out and practiced jumps. That might be cool. But he wasn't ready to give up his attitude. "So, we're all going to be crammed together in this house. What about Santa Paws and Cookie? Nobody's ever going to let *them* stay with us. They're going to have to go to a kennel."

Under the table, Santa Paws let out a little whimper. He had no idea what a kennel was, but by the sound of Gregory's voice, it was *not* a good thing.

"When have we *ever* put a pet in a kennel?" asked Mrs. Callahan. "Of course they're coming with us. Just the dogs, though. We'll get a house sitter to stay with the cats."

"Yay!" Miranda yelled. "Cookie's coming!"

Cookie jumped up and went over to kiss Miranda.

"I think it'll be wonderful," said Mrs. Callahan. "I've been dying to try out those snowshoes I got last Christmas."

"That's what I want to do, too," said Emily. "Just wander in the woods, following animal tracks, drinking in the quiet . . ." She looked at her daughters. "Well, maybe it won't be *that* quiet with Lucy in a sled and Miranda snowshoeing along with us, but, anyway, we'll be out there in the great outdoors."

"And I'll get a real vacation, for the first time in years," said Steve. "Plus, I'll get to see all my old buddies." Growing up, Steve had been on the ski patrol at North Woods. Every winter, he'd spent all his free time skiing — and helping injured skiers. Gregory and Patricia had heard lots of stories about those "good old days."

"I'm just going to hang out, though," said Steve. "No skiing. I haven't done it in years, and I don't want to get hurt. But I do miss patrolling at the valley. I think patrolling was what first made me think of being a policeman," Steve reflected. "I liked helping people, making sure they were safe."

"Well, all your plans sound fine," said Mr. Callahan. "But I'm not interested in flying down hills or tromping through the woods in the freezing cold. I'll be spending *my* time by the fire, catching up on my reading and napping. I hear there's a great hot tub at this B and B, too. A little soaking now and then will complete my relaxation."

Gregory and Patricia had been listening to all of this, exchanging glances now and then. "Well," Patricia finally said, leaning back in her chair with her arms crossed. "I'm glad *you're* all psyched for this trip. Just don't expect me and Gregory to be jumping up and down with happiness. We had our own plans for vacation."

"Such as?" her mother asked, raising an eyebrow.

"Such as being *here*," Patricia said.

"Doing stuff with our friends," Gregory agreed.

"Hanging out. Chilling," Patricia added.

"So, then, doing what you always do?" asked Mr. Callahan. "Sounds exciting."

"Anyway, the decision's been made," said Mrs. Callahan firmly, getting up to start clearing the table. "I'm sure we'll all have a wonderful time."

Gregory and Santa Paws headed back to Gregory's room after dinner. Santa Paws lay on the rug, thinking happily about all the pizza crusts he'd eaten. Gregory lay on his bed, sulking a little.

He knew that going to Vermont for Christmas wasn't the *worst* thing he could be forced to do, but he didn't like the way his parents had made the decision without even consulting him. After all, he wasn't six anymore.

Half an hour later, Patricia burst into his room, grinning like a fool. "Guess what," she said. "Rachel's coming with us!" She plopped herself down on Gregory's bed and told him the whole story. "I just found out that Rachel's family is going to Vermont for Christmas, too, but they're going to Stowe, and they're not going until Christmas Day. So I asked Mom and Dad, and she's coming up with us a few days early. Her parents will pick her up. Isn't that cool?"

Gregory eyed his sister. "Cool for you," he said, knowing that having her best friend along would make Patricia happy. "Is Spike coming?"

Spike was Rachel's golden retriever, a guide

dog. Rachel was blind and, until recently, had gotten around with a cane. Now that she had Spike, her world had grown.

Patricia shook her head. "Rachel says he needs a little update on some of his training, so he's going to stick around here while she and her parents are on vacation."

"Lucky Spike," Gregory muttered. His mood was not improved by his sister's news.

Santa Paws sensed that Gregory was upset. The dog nudged the boy's hand with his nose. "That's right, big guy," Gregory said, leaning over to give the dog a pat. "At least I'll have you along. That counts for a lot."

3

"Should be smooth sailing, according to Weather.com!" Tom Callahan said, as he opened the door for his brother.

"You've been online already?" asked Steve, shaking his head. "It's five a.m., for Pete's sake."

Santa Paws looked from one Callahan brother to the other. The dog knew that something was different: This morning was not starting out like most regular mornings. It was dark, for one thing. The sun wouldn't be up for a long time. There was a stack of suitcases, skis, poles, ski boots, snowshoes, and winter boots in the hall, for another. And Tom had turned on his computer before he had even entered the kitchen.

Santa Paws waited patiently for Mr. Callahan to realize that, different or not, it was morning and that meant it was time for breakfast.

Cookie was still snoozing in Patricia's room. Gregory, Patricia, and Eileen were asleep, too. But that wouldn't last long, the way Tom and

Steve were bumping around. They began to drag suitcases outside to Steve's maroon minivan and the Callahans' station wagon.

"No snow in the forecast at all," Tom said. "The temperature is going to be dropping throughout the day today, but that shouldn't be a problem. And since we're getting such an early start, there won't be any traffic, either."

"I hope Emily and the girls appreciate that I let them sleep in for an extra half hour while I came over to pack," grumbled Steve. "Emily promised to have breakfast ready when we go back to pick them up."

At the word "breakfast," Santa Paws's ears perked up. He looked hopefully at Mr. Callahan and took a few steps toward his dish. He may have even let out a small bark.

Tom got the hint. "Right, Santa Paws," he said. "Sorry about that. Let's get you some kibble."

The rattle of kibble hitting the metal dog dish woke Cookie, all the way upstairs, and brought her flying into the kitchen. Tom fed her, too. Then he and Steve finished carrying all the gear out to the cars.

"I'll rouse the troops," Tom told his brother. "We'll be over in fifteen minutes. Tell Emily we'll stop at the bakery and pick up some cinnamon rolls."

* * *

28

One hour, two pots of coffee, a dozen cinnamon rolls, and a few rounds of pancakes later, the Callahan convoy was on the move. Though they hadn't exactly planned it that way, the passengers had divided into a girls' car (Emily, Eileen, Patricia, Rachel, Lucy, Miranda, and Cookie in Steve and Emily's minivan) and a boys' car (Tom, Gregory, Steve, and Santa Paws in the Callahans' station wagon, along with a tangle of skis, poles, and other gear).

Gregory was happy to let his father drive. Still groggy from his early wake-up call, he sprawled in the backseat, leaning against the warm soft body of Santa Paws. The dog was alert as always, watching out the window as the car whizzed through the landscape, heading north as the sun began to rise.

Behind them in the minivan, Cookie was curled up on the seat between the younger girls' car seats, resting peacefully in the knowledge that she was close to Miranda, her favorite person in the world. Patricia and Rachel sat in the far backseat, dozing and listening to music, Patricia on her Discman and Rachel on her iPod. Mrs. Callahan and Emily talked softly as Emily drove the van, following the station wagon along the almost empty early-morning highway.

"How much longer?" Gregory asked his father, rubbing his eyes.

"About, what, two and a half hours?" Mr.

Callahan asked his brother. "We just crossed the Vermont border."

"We're making great time," said Steve. He stretched and yawned. "Man, it feels so good to be on vacation," he said. "I can't remember the last time I took off more than one day in a row."

In the backseat, Santa Paws yawned, too, letting out a noisy sigh.

Steve laughed. "You, too, Santa Paws?"

"Santa Paws does deserve a vacation," said Gregory. "Christmas is usually his busiest time for helping people, but maybe this year will be different."

"At least he won't have to deal with all his fans," said Mr. Callahan. Santa Paws had done so many amazing things over the years that his fame had spread throughout Oceanport and beyond. The dog even got fan mail! Not that it meant much to him, except for the rare letter in which someone enclosed a Milk-Bone. But up in the woods of Vermont, he would probably go unrecognized for once.

"I wouldn't count on that," Steve said. "My old patrolling buddies know all about him. Mark and Andy can't wait to meet the world-famous rescue dog."

Mark and Andy were two of the patrollers Steve had worked with at North Woods. Both of them were still on the ski patrol there. They had heard about Santa Paws after one of his first amazing rescues, when he helped Gregory and Patricia find their way out of the deep forests and steep, snow-filled ravines of New Hampshire's White Mountains. The Callahan kids and Santa Paws had been flying to Vermont one Christmas years ago when the small plane Steve piloted crashed. Steve was badly injured, and Santa Paws and the two children — Gregory was only eleven at the time — had managed to make their way to civilization to get help.

Steve had pretty much given up flying after that. He reached back to scratch Santa Paws's ears. "You're the man," he told Santa Paws. "The two of us are going to enjoy this vacation to the max."

"The two of you aren't the only ones," said Mr. Callahan. "I know my work may not be as physically demanding as yours, but my brain does get tired once in a while. I need to recharge my batteries."

"Me, too," said Gregory. "But I could have done that at home, without having to get up at the crack of dawn and drive for a million hours." He was actually starting to look forward to this vacation, but he wasn't quite ready to let his father and uncle off the hook for planning it without consulting him.

"Try *five* hours," his father said mildly.

"Whatever," said Gregory. He sat back and crossed his arms, looking out the window at the forested landscape. There was already more snow on the ground here than at home. That was promising. Maybe this would be the year that he would get really, really good at snowboarding. He'd never had the chance before to spend more than a day or two at a time practicing.

Up front, Steve turned to his brother. "You know what I was thinking about the other day?" he asked. "Those songs Dad used to sing to us when we went on car trips, back when we were kids. I was trying to sing them to the girls, but I couldn't remember all the words."

"You mean songs like 'A Horse Named Bill'?" asked Mr. Callahan, smiling.

"Exactly!" cried Steve. "Do you remember the words?"

Gregory groaned. His father had a knack for remembering the words to songs. Usually, he sang Frank Sinatra songs, but he could get going on Beatles songs, too, or even horrendous seventies stuff like the Bee Gees. "Dad —" he said, hoping to change the subject quickly.

But it was too late. Mr. Callahan had already begun to sing.

"Oh, I had a horse, his name was Bill.
When he ran, he couldn't stand still."
He sang to the tune of "Dixie."

"He ran away, one day, and also
I ran with him."

"That's it!" Steve cried, joining in, and the brothers sang together.

> "He ran so fast he could not stop,
> He ran into a barber shop
> And fell exhaustionized, with his
> eyeteeth
> In the barber's left shoulder."

Gregory laughed. He couldn't help himself. The song was so silly! He kind of remembered hearing Granddad sing the song, years ago. Santa Paws leaned into Gregory and licked his face. The dog felt better now that Gregory was laughing instead of frowning. A frowning Gregory was no fun to be around. And a frowning Gregory hardly ever handed out Milk-Bones.

Up front, the brothers continued to sing.

> "Oh, I had a gal, her name was Daisy,
> When she sang, the cats went crazy,
> With deliriums, Saint Vituses, and all kinds of
> cataleptics."

They cracked themselves up, laughing so hard they couldn't sing for a few moments.

"What's next?" asked Steve. "Something about a river, I remember."

Mr. Callahan didn't pause.

"One day she sang a song about
A man who turned himself inside out —"

Steve joined in again, laughing, and the two finished the song together.

"And jumped into the river,
He was so very sleepy."

The brothers were on a roll by then.
"Oooh," they chorused loudly.

"I went up in a balloon so big,
The people on the earth they looked like
    a pig —
Like a mice, like a geese, like fleases —"

"Dad!" Gregory said. "Uncle Steve!" His voice was urgent. "Stop singing! Something's wrong."

Beside Gregory, Santa Paws had stiffened to attention. His nose was in the air. His ears were on full alert. He stood on the car seat, facing forward, whining softly.

There was trouble ahead. The dog could sense it.

The singing stopped.

Steve glanced back at the dog, then looked ahead, up the road. "Whoa!" he shouted, his voice suddenly very serious. "Pull over! Now!"

4

"I'm trying!" said Mr. Callahan, wrenching the steering wheel. "The car doesn't want to steer!"

Suddenly, the station wagon was veering all over the highway, sliding out of control as it fishtailed back and forth.

"Black ice!" shouted Steve. "Go with the skid. Steer *into* it."

Mr. Callahan held on for dear life, spinning the steering wheel in the direction of the sliding car. For one terrifying moment, the car spun all the way around, and Gregory could see the maroon minivan behind them, sliding sideways along the road. They were close enough to it so he could see his mother's horrified face, and Emily's hands clenched on the wheel.

Gregory put his arms around Santa Paws and held on tight. "We'll be okay, big guy," he said into the dog's ear. "We'll be okay."

The dog did not relax a single muscle. This

was bad. This was very bad. The car just *had* to stop sliding soon. There was danger ahead.

In the minivan, Cookie had woken from her nap. She peered between the two front seats, watching as the landscape slid by in a dizzying swirl. Then she looked up at Miranda.

"Mommy!" cried Miranda. "What's happening? I'm scared! Stop the car! Stop it!" She began to cry. Lucy joined in.

Patricia leaned forward to put a hand on each of her young cousins' shoulders. "It's okay," she said, as soothingly as she could manage. "Hang on. It's going to be okay." She whispered to Rachel. "We're spinning. But we're slowing down. We'll be all right."

Up front, Emily gripped the wheel, trying to remember everything she knew about how to deal with a skid. When they had first bought the minivan, she and Steve had taken it out to a snowy parking lot and practiced so she could get the feel for how to steer it in slippery conditions. She could almost hear his voice in her ear: "Steer into the skid," he would say. "Stay relaxed. Don't tense up. Don't slam on the brakes. Just go with it."

Eileen Callahan sat next to her, holding on to her armrest so hard that her knuckles turned white. She watched the station wagon in front of them sail from one side of the road to the other, spinning around at one point so that she could see Gregory's white face staring back at hers.

It all seemed to happen in slow motion. Finally, the station wagon slid off the road and into the snow-packed median strip, where it came to rest. The minivan slid past it a little way, then likewise plowed slowly into a snowbank.

Mrs. Callahan gasped. "Is everyone all right?" she asked, turning around in her seat.

Emily let out a huge breath and took her hands from the wheel. "I'm okay," she said. "Miranda? Lucy?"

"M-m-mommy!" cried Miranda. "I want you!" She held out her arms. Beside her, Lucy wailed loudly.

Emily unbuckled her seat belt and slid between the two front seats to hug her girls.

"Patricia? Rachel?" Mrs. Callahan took off her belt, too.

"We're fine," Patricia said. "Right, Rach? We're absolutely fine." Then she burst into tears.

Behind them, in the station wagon, Tom Callahan was sitting with a dazed look, his hands still on the steering wheel.

"You okay?" Steve asked his brother softly. "You did a good job."

Tom nodded.

"Gregory?" Steve asked, turning in his seat. "You all right? And the dog?"

"We're good," Gregory said, his voice a little choked. "What happened?"

Next to him, Santa Paws whined softly. He was still on full alert, every muscle tensed. The horrible sliding had stopped, but the danger was not over. Something was still very, very wrong. Somebody needed his help.

"Black ice," Steve explained. "It happens sometimes when there's melted snow on the roadway, and then the temperature drops. The road looks dry, but there are these patches of sheer ice you can't even see. Once you hit one, you're out of control." As he spoke, he was unbuckling his seat belt. "I'm going to check on the others," he said. "I see movement in the van, so I think they're all fine. You guys stay here in the car where it's safe." The policeman in Steve took over at times like these.

"Okay, Steve," said Mr. Callahan. "Just — be careful."

"Yeah," said Gregory. "Be careful."

"Of course," said Steve. He opened the car door and stepped out. Before he could slam it shut, a brown blur shot out of the backseat and flew past him, out of the car.

"Santa Paws! No! Stay!" Steve shouted.

"Come back, Santa Paws!" yelled Mr. Callahan.

Gregory knew there was no point in trying to call his dog back. When Santa Paws sensed trouble, he was determined to find it — and to help. There was no stopping him. Gregory pushed open his door and climbed out.

"Gregory! I told you to stay in the car," Steve said.

"Can't," said Gregory, taking off after his dog. "I'll be careful!" he yelled back, over his shoulder. At least it was still early enough so there were hardly any other cars or trucks to spin out and hurt the dog, but Gregory wasn't about to let him run down the road alone.

Steve raced to the van. "Everybody all right in here?" he asked, opening the passenger-side door.

"We're fine," said Mrs. Callahan. "But —"

"We're all fine, too," Steve said. "Listen. Stay put. Santa Paws is up to something, and we need to go find out what it is. You're safest in the van, for now." He looked past Mrs. Callahan to his wife. "You're really okay?" he asked her.

"I'm really okay," she said. "We all are."

He smiled a quick smile. "Okay. Give me the cell phone. We'll be back as soon as we can. Don't let Cookie out, whatever you do! One dog on the highway is enough."

Cookie heard her name. She had seen Santa Paws race past the van, but right this minute she had no urge to join him. Her place was with Miranda and the others. Maybe she could distract them, make them laugh. That would be good. Everybody was being so serious. Cookie didn't like that.

Emily handed the cell phone to Steve. "Be careful," she said. "I mean it."

"I know you do," said Steve. "Don't worry. We'll be right back." He blew kisses to his wife and daughters — and to Patricia and Rachel in the backseat. "Hang in there, girls," he said.

"Take care of Gregory!" said Mrs. Callahan.

"Of course," Steve said. Then he shut the van door and began running after Santa Paws.

The boy and his dog were already out of sight, up over a slight rise. Steve ran along the side of the road, crunching through the snow so that he wouldn't slip on the ice-slicked road. Behind him, he heard a car horn wail as another vehicle slid on the ice. He turned briefly, just long enough to see a white Subaru come to rest on the other side of the highway from the van and station wagon. Good. They were safe.

As he ran, Steve began to dial 911 on the cell phone. When the dispatcher picked up, Steve gasped out, "Multiple vehicles off the highway on I-91, northbound between exits two and three. Let the troopers know they should close the road. Black ice."

He crested the hill just then and spotted Santa Paws running down the other side. Gregory was right behind him. Still, there was nothing in

40

sight. The road was empty — something to be grateful for, Steve thought. Another small hill lay in front of them. Steve kept running, trying to catch up.

Suddenly, Santa Paws stopped short at the bottom of the hill, near a ditch. He lowered his head and sniffed. The hair on the back of his neck stood up. Then he turned to face Gregory and began to bark. Loud warning barks. It was a bad smell, a dangerous smell. Gregory and Steve had to stay back.

Gregory didn't stop running. In fact, he sped up. "What is it, Santa Paws?" That barking had to mean something. Gregory sprinted the last fifty yards, closing the distance between himself and Santa Paws. The cold air seared his lungs as he charged toward the dog, his shoes punching holes in the snow. When he finally reached the dog, he leaned over, hands on knees, head down, gasping for breath.

With his head lower, Gregory could suddenly smell what the dog smelled. It was a skunky odor that made his nose wrinkle up. "What's that?" he asked out loud, just as his uncle caught up with him, breathing hard.

"Oh, no!" Steve said, bending low for a sniff. "Propane!"

Steve's mind flashed back to his HazMat training at the police academy, when he'd learned all about handling accidents that involved hazardous materials. Propane was an odorless gas, he remembered. The companies that sold it added a chemical that gave it that skunky smell, so that leaks could be detected. What was that stuff called? Methyl something. Anyway, the odor was unmistakable. And the reason they could only smell it when their heads were down low was because propane, like many gases, hugged the ground and low spots when it leaked. It must be traveling along the ditch at his feet. Steve remembered what to do when you found a big propane leak. You had to keep people out of low areas and move them as far away as possible.

Steve glanced back down the road, thinking of all the people he loved in those two cars. Thankfully, there was a hill between them and this leaking gas. With luck, the gas would not find its way to the station wagon and minivan. The fumes could be dangerous on their own, and if they were ignited — he didn't want to think about that.

But what about the truck? There must have been a truck carrying the propane, and it must have slid off the road. And the driver?

"Gregory, stay here. Stay, Santa Paws," Steve commanded, knowing it was probably hopeless to expect the dog — or the boy — to obey. Sure enough, when Steve began to run again, the dog took off, too, galloping so fast that he left Steve and Gregory behind almost immediately. Gregory took after his dog like a shot.

Santa Paws stopped at the crest of the hill and looked down. There, across the median on the opposite side of the highway, was a truck on its side. No other cars or trucks were nearby. Santa Paws looked back at Steve and Gregory and barked loud, harsh barks. They must not come any closer!

Santa Paws knew there was no time to waste. With every ounce of energy in his strong, muscular body, he bounded across the median toward the overturned truck. As he drew near, he saw the figure of a man, crawling slowly across the ice-slicked road. The driver! Santa Paws ran as fast as he could. The man had to move faster! He had to get away from the truck before something terrible happened!

As he dashed toward the crashed truck, Santa Paws began to slip and slide on the icy road. He stiffened his legs and spread his paws, trying to get traction. His toenails dug into the road, scratching at the icy surface.

Gregory watched in horror. "Be careful, Santa Paws!" he cried. He watched as his dog slid right into the man. Santa Paws needed his help! The boy ran faster until he got to the slick road and tried to follow Santa Paws across the icy asphalt. It was no use. He slipped and fell immediately and had to retreat to the edge of the road. Steve had just arrived. He and Steve stood helplessly, watching Santa Paws.

"What —" the man asked in a fuzzy voice. A gash on his forehead oozed blood into one eye, and his gaze was unfocused.

Santa Paws grabbed the man's collar in his teeth and began to tug, slipping and sliding as he dragged the man across the slippery road. The man groaned. "Stop!" he mumbled. "I can walk. I can get there myself!"

Santa Paws didn't listen. He just kept adjusting his jaws, keeping hold of the man's collar as he pulled him, inch by exhausting inch, toward the median where Gregory and Steve stood. Finally, he felt the crunch of snow beneath his paws. He loosened his grip on the man's collar for a moment and looked up.

Gregory patted his head. "Good boy, Santa Paws. Good work."

Steve nodded. "Let's get this guy as far away from the truck as we can." He bent to grab the man by the arm. "Come on. You're in shock, but you have to come with me. There's a possibility your truck may explode, or that a ruptured tank could rocket toward us."

Santa Paws, Gregory, and Steve tugged the man along, pulling him through the snow until they were a hundred yards from the truck.

"Okay," said Steve. "Far enough for the moment. Let me call this in." He dialed 911 again on the cell phone. "We need a hazardous materials response team," he told the dispatcher, gasping a little as he tried to recover his breath. "I-91, southbound. Near exit two. Propane truck. Placard number is 1075. Company name: Agway. Saddle fuel tanks look intact, no diesel leakage likely." Steve knew that the propane company would have its own emergency technicians, trained in how to deal with an accident with one of their trucks. The number he'd given them — which he'd seen on the red, diamond-shaped sign on the truck — would tell them everything they needed to know about what was leaking and what the dangers were.

"Until we have an incident commander," he went on, "tell the troopers to close I-91, north- and southbound. HazMat regulations say we need to secure the area and ensure scene safety. If there are houses within eight hundred yards, we may have to evacuate."

Steve gave the dispatcher a few more details, then hung up. Just then, the truck driver groaned and stirred. "Can you walk?" Steve asked the man. "I need to assess your injuries, but the most important thing right now is to get away from the truck. We'll get you over to our cars. I have some first-aid supplies there, and an ambulance will be here soon."

With Steve on one side of the man and Gregory on the other, the three made their way back over the hill. Santa Paws ran back and forth anxiously, making sure everyone was all right. When they came into view, Mr. Callahan waved at them. "The troopers were just here!" he shouted. "They've gone back to shut off the exit, but they're on the case."

Sirens sounded in the distance. Steve and Gregory looked at each other as they arrived at the minivan, the truck driver staggering between them. "I thought I told you to stay in the car," Steve said to his nephew, trying to sound stern.

"I couldn't let Santa Paws go alone," Gregory answered.

"I know," Steve said quietly. "Thanks. You did well out there."

Then Steve looked down at the dog with a tired grin. "Some vacation, huh, Santa Paws?"

5

"Welcome, welcome! Please, come in." The woman opened the door wide. "I am Thea, your host. We are so happy to have you staying with us."

She was tall, with shining brown hair, a broad smile, and a Dutch accent. She pronounced her name "Tay-a." The door she opened was painted a vivid blue, and the room it opened into was warm, bright, and as welcoming as she was.

The Callahans had finally arrived at their slope-side B and B — much later than they had intended. Once they had finished dealing with the accident on the highway, it had taken hours to work their way north on smaller roads; the interstate had remained closed to traffic. It was late afternoon by the time they drove up the steep, winding access road to North Woods.

The ski area was like a little village. It was a group of snow-covered buildings clustered at the base of the mountain, with a hotel, a lodge, restaurants, a deli, a ski shop, and a big sports center that housed a pool, sauna, and gym. Two chairlifts, a rope tow, and a gondola serviced the trails on the mountainside. Some trails were wide open and others wound their way through deep woods, but they all made a pretty white tracery against the mountain's face. Seeing it all again, Gregory started to get excited. North Woods was a separate world, a special place that was all about winter fun.

The Winterhaus B and B was tucked into a grove of pine trees. Its multiple balconies were decorated with white Christmas lights and evergreen wreaths with big red bows. Before they began bringing in all their baggage, Tom Callahan introduced himself and the rest of the family to Thea and her husband, Dan.

Dan helped them get oriented. "This trail behind the house is a snowmobile trail," he said. "If you follow it to the left up the hill, you'll come to the snowshoe trails that wander all over the undeveloped side of the mountain. If you follow it down the hill, it winds around to the North Woods main lodge."

"And these are your dogs?" asked Thea, bending down to greet Santa Paws and Cookie. "Hello, handsome," she said to Santa Paws, as she rubbed his ears. "And aren't you a funny one?" she asked Cookie, shaking the paw that Cookie offered. "Welcome to both of you."

She straightened up. "Your parents," she said to Tom and Steve, "said they will see you tomorrow. They suggest you relax tonight and get settled in."

"What about dinner?" asked Emily. "Is there a restaurant at the resort?"

"Of course," said Thea. "But for tonight, we hope you'll join us for a family meal. Just soup and bread and cheese, nothing fancy."

Mrs. Callahan sighed happily. "That sounds *perfect*," she said.

"Let me show you to your rooms," said Thea, leading the way up a flight of stairs. "We have put the two youngest girls in the yellow room, and their parents in the green room right next door," she said.

"Yay!" said Miranda. "Yellow is my favorite color!"

"No, mine!" said Lucy, whose favorite color changed every five minutes lately.

"Here is one bathroom." Thea continued the tour. "And a sitting room, with books and games and such."

"And a very comfortable-looking couch, right next to the fireplace," observed Tom Callahan with satisfaction. "This is my spot."

"Perfect!" said Thea. "Your room is right across the hall, the red room." She opened the door and showed Mr. and Mrs. Callahan their cozy, bright room.

"And the three older children will have their own little wing," Thea finished, turning a corner as she led the way down another hall. She showed Patricia and Rachel the blue room, which had two double beds covered in thick down quilts and a window seat looking out at pine trees.

"It's gorgeous," Patricia told Rachel. She described the room for her friend. "Blue velvet curtains, blue-and-white floral wallpaper, and a dark blue carpet. You can have the bed closest to the door. It's straight ahead, at twelve o'clock."

Thea took Gregory down the hall to show him the gold room, which was just past the bathroom he would share with Patricia and Rachel. Santa Paws padded into the room after Gregory, eyeing the rug next to the bed.

"Would your dog like to sleep in here?" Thea asked.

"Can he?" asked Gregory.

"Sure," said Thea. "We have a very soft and comfortable dog bed he'll love. I'll have Dan bring it up. And the other dog?"

"She'll probably want to sleep in Miranda's room," Gregory told her. "Or maybe Patricia's."

"We will give her a bed to use as well," Thea said, smiling.

After the tour, everyone gathered in the sitting room for a moment. "So," said Thea, "take your time settling in, then come down to the dining room for some supper. And afterward, try the hot tub." She headed off down the stairs.

"Wow," said Mr. Callahan. "Nice digs."

"Huh?" asked Miranda, looking around. "Did Santa Paws dig a hole?"

Everybody laughed. "It's just an expression," explained Mr. Callahan. "It means this place seems perfect for us. We can really relax and enjoy our vacation now."

"I sure hope so," sighed Steve.

Santa Paws sighed, too. He lay down near the fireplace, hoping for a quick nap. It had been a long day, and he was tired. But he jumped right up again when Gregory and the others headed downstairs to unload the cars. He and Cookie supervised as the family brought in all their things. Then Gregory and Patricia took Cookie and Santa Paws for a short walk along the snowmobile trail. Santa Paws trotted along, enjoying the feeling of the packed snow beneath his paws and the smell of the pine trees lining the trail. Cookie darted back and forth, sniffing wildly at the marvelous new scents. Both dogs were excited to be in this pretty new place with the people they loved.

Later, after a satisfying meal of split-pea soup and grilled cheese sandwiches, Tom Callahan pushed back his chair. "Perfect," he said. "Thank you, Thea and Dan. And now, I'm off to check out that hot tub. Anyone care to join me?"

"Not me," said Emily. "I'm going to get these little bugs to bed." She put an arm around each of her daughters' shoulders.

"Not me," said Eileen. "I have a brand-new mystery novel I'm dying to get into. I'm headed for the sitting room."

"Not me," said Gregory. He held up a North Woods brochure he'd been looking at. "I'm going tubing!"

"Tubing?" asked Patricia. "Isn't that something you do on a river? Seems like it'd be pretty icy right now."

"*Snow* tubing, smarty-pants," said Gregory. "They have night tubing here. You can take the rope tow up the mountain with your tube, and then you slide down. The slope is all lit up, and there's music, and it's like a big party."

"Gee, I hate to miss it," said Mr. Callahan insincerely. "Too bad I have big plans to soak until I look like a prune."

"I'm game," said Rachel.

"Me, too," Patricia said quickly.

"I'll go with you," said Steve. "They never had tubing back in my day. Sounds like fun."

After they'd given Santa Paws and Cookie dinner and settled the dogs in for the night, Gregory, Patricia, Rachel, and Steve put on their ski pants and jackets. Dan told them which way to go for the tubing park. "During the day, you can ski over to that lift. But at night it's easier to drive. Park at the bottom of the hill. You'll know which way to go when you hear the music."

Sure enough, the tubing park was obvious as soon as they got out of the station wagon. Music was blasting. Huge, overgrown streetlights that bounced their glare off the snow made it look like high noon. And dozens of people were riding up the rope tow and flying back down the hill on their tubes, screaming and laughing as they careened down the four long, banked runs that took up the whole wide slope.

"Awesome!" said Gregory. "Let's go!"

"Uh," Steve hesitated. "I don't know. Looks kind of dangerous, don't you think?"

"Are you kidding?" asked Patricia, who was busy describing the scene to Rachel. "It looks like the most fun ever. Rachel's up for it, and she can't even see!"

"Maybe that's why she's up for it," Steve said drily. "Anyway, you guys go ahead. I think I just spotted someone I know over there." He pointed to a man wearing a red jacket with a big white cross on the back, standing near the bottom of the slope.

Gregory charged over to the bottom of the rope tow. Patricia and Rachel ran after him. But as Gregory got closer to the lift, he slowed down.

"What's the matter, chickening out?" Patricia asked, panting a little as she caught up with him.

"No way," Gregory said. "I'm just checking out

how to do this." He and Patricia watched as people lined up for the lift. Three boys about Gregory's age were just getting on. The first one sat down in his tube, facing downhill. He handed the tube's strap to the lift attendant, who hooked it onto the lift rope.

"Later!" the boy said, waving to his friends. They followed in their own tubes.

"Got it," said Gregory. "No problem." He grabbed a tube, hopped on, and gave the loop to the attendant. "See you at the top!" he called to Patricia, who was describing the routine to Rachel.

Gregory held on tight as the tube slid magically uphill. His heart was beating fast. This was going to be so cool! He craned his neck around to see how far he was from the top. Then, suddenly, he realized something. He didn't really know what to do when he got there! How would the tube get unhooked from the rope? His heart started to beat even faster.

Down at the bottom, Patricia and Rachel were talking to the lift attendant. Rachel was explaining that she might need a little extra help since she couldn't see, and the attendant was explaining how they should hop out of their still-moving tubes as they came to the top.

"Oh, man," Gregory moaned, as the tube neared the top of the lift. He craned his neck again and watched as the three boys ahead of him hopped neatly out of their tubes, grabbing the straps as the attendant unhooked them.

Gregory took a deep breath. "I can do that," he said. He got ready to jump as the tube neared the top of the lift. "One, two, three," he counted under his breath. Then he launched. And fell. Hard.

The three boys were watching. They laughed. Then one of them came over to Gregory. "Nice face-plant," he said, handing Gregory his tube. "I did the same thing my first time." He was skinny and tall, with long blond hair.

"Is it that obvious that it's my first time?" Gregory asked, grinning.

"Come on," said the boy. "We'll show you the best lane. I'm Tyler."

"Gregory. What do you mean, the best lane?"

"Best, like fastest. Lane Four," said one of the other boys, who was wearing a black knit cap with a skull and crossbones on it. "Dude, it's wicked fast." He nodded to Gregory. "I'm Jason. And that's Frogger." He pointed at the third boy, who was wearing a backward baseball cap and baggy snowboarding pants.

Gregory looked down the hill to see if Patricia and Rachel were on their way up. They were still nearly at the bottom. Should he wait for them?

"C'mon," said Frogger. "The lift closes in half an hour. We have to get in as many runs as we can." He and his friends started toward the slope.

"Wait up," said Gregory, deciding to forget about Patricia and Rachel. After all, they had each other. He took off after the boys, watching them closely as they ran to the top of the lanes, flopped down on their tubes, and flew down the hill, bouncing off the sides of the lane and whooping loudly. Gregory raced down after them.

At the bottom of the hill, he rolled off his tube, laughing so hard he couldn't catch his breath. "That was totally wack!" he shouted.

Then he saw his uncle Steve and the man in the red coat coming toward him.

"Yo, guys," said the ski patroller. "No running starts. You know the rules." He pointed to a big sign near the bottom of the slope.

No RUNNING STARTS.
TUBE IN CONTROL.
ONE TUBE AT A TIME IN EACH LANE.
No PINBALLING.

"Oops," Gregory said, almost to himself. He'd broken all the rules on his first run. "Sorry. It was my first time."

"You're excused," said the patroller, winking at him. "But your friends here know better."

Tyler shrugged. "Whatever," he said. He picked up his tube and headed for the lift. Jason and Frogger followed him, and Gregory started to. But Steve stopped him.

"Hold on, Gregory," he said. "I want you to meet my friend Mark."

"Heard a lot about you," Mark said, sticking out his hand for a shake. "It's not every kid who could save his uncle after a plane crash."

"I didn't save anybody," Gregory mumbled. "It was Santa Paws."

"Oh, yes, the famous dog," said Mark. "Can't wait to meet him." He looked down at Gregory, serious for a moment. "Listen," he said. "Watch out for those guys. They take risks, and they're going to get their passes yanked one of these days."

"Passes?" asked Gregory.

"They're locals," said Mark. "They have season passes. They're here all the time, and they think they own the place. They're not really bad kids. They're just a little cocky. So — be careful around them, okay?"

"Sure," said Gregory. He looked over at the rope tow. He was dying for another run.

"Go ahead," said Steve. "I'll be hanging out down here. Mark's trying to talk me into skiing with him tomorrow, and I'm trying to explain that I *like* not having any broken legs."

Gregory laughed. Then he took off like a shot, running to catch up with his new friends. Maybe this vacation wasn't going to be such a drag after all.

6

The dog woke suddenly when Gregory swung his feet over the side of the bed. Where was he? It took a moment for him to remember. He was in a new place, but he was with his family. All was well. He had slept deeply on the soft, warm bed next to Gregory's bed. Now it was morning. The room was filled with sunshine that bounced off the snow covering everything outside the windows. That meant one thing. Breakfast time! It would not be long before someone — probably Mrs. Callahan — put down a big dish full of kibble for him to gobble up.

Or maybe there would be something special for breakfast! Santa Paws leapt to his feet. Last night, the nice lady whose house this seemed to be had given him one of the best biscuits he had ever had. "I make these myself," he had heard her tell Mr. Callahan. "All our dog guests seem to love them."

Cookie, of course, had turned up her nose at

the dog biscuit and had been given an oatmeal-raisin cookie instead — also homemade.

"Hey, buddy," Gregory said, giving Santa Paws an affectionate ear rub. "You missed all the fun last night. Too bad dogs aren't allowed on the slopes." Gregory could hardly wait to get out onto the snow again. He had made plans to meet Tyler, Jason, and Frogger for some snowboarding.

"We know this mountain like it was our own backyard," Tyler had boasted. "We'll show you places nobody else even knows about."

Gregory was just the tiniest bit nervous about where those guys were going to take him — and whether he'd be able to keep up with them — but his excitement outweighed his anxiety.

Down the hall, Patricia was telling Rachel that it was a beautiful morning. "The sky is bright blue," she reported, "and all the trees are covered in snow. Conditions should be perfect for skiing."

Rachel was rummaging in her suitcase. "Can you help me find my vest?" she asked. "I know my mom put it in here. She's so worried about me skiing without it."

Patricia reached in and pulled out a bright orange piece of material that said BLIND SKIER. "Here it is," she said. "It was folded up inside your helmet. We're all set." She had learned all about adaptive skiing from being friends with Rachel. It was so cool that anyone could learn to ski: blind people, hearing-impaired people, even people who had been paralyzed or had legs amputated. There were techniques and equipment for just about every disability you could think of. Last winter, she and Rachel had gone to a workshop for blind skiers, and Patricia had learned all about how to ski with Rachel, calling out directions and warning her about potential hazards in her path.

Rachel had been so game! The instructors started her off slowly, having her wear just one ski at first and scooting along on a flat area, then adding the other ski so she could get a sense of how that felt. Within hours, Rachel had been swooping downhill, yelling happily. "I feel like I'm flying!" she'd shouted.

Patricia wondered if she'd be able to do the same if she were blind. Once, she had kept her eyes closed while she got onto the chairlift, just to see how it felt to Rachel. It was terrifying! She'd felt herself get scooped up and carried along at what seemed like twice the usual speed.

Tubing the night before had been a blast. After getting special permission from the patrollers, she had held on to the strap on Rachel's tube so they could go down the run together. Each time, they had gone a little faster, screaming and yelling as they shot down the slope.

Skiing should be even more fun, Patricia thought as she pulled on her pink-and-purple-striped long underwear.

Soon the smell of bacon and freshly baked bread began to creep upstairs, and before long the entire Callahan clan was gathered in the dining room downstairs. Cookie bounced back and forth between the table and the kitchen door, following Thea as she delivered platter after platter of delicious food to the table. "Didn't you just have breakfast?" Thea asked, shaking her head at Cookie's antics. "Okay, okay, one cookie for you. I can't resist that face."

Cookie didn't understand the words, but she was happy to accept the treat Thea offered — a peanut butter cookie that smelled SO much better than those silly biscuits Santa Paws was so crazy about. Cookie crept under the table and demolished her treat at Miranda's feet.

"Let's try that Maple Loop trail," Emily said to Eileen, as they pored over a map of the snowshoe trails after breakfast. "Thea says she's seen all kinds of animal tracks in that area."

"Sounds good to me," said Mrs. Callahan. "Sure you don't want to come, honey?" She looked over at her husband.

"Love to," said Tom Callahan. "But somebody has to hold down the fort."

"Hold down the couch is more like it," Gregory muttered. "I give him about fifteen minutes before he falls asleep."

"I heard that!" said Mr. Callahan, grinning. "Make it twenty. I promised the dogs a walk before I lie down."

"How about you, Steve?" asked Mrs. Callahan. "Did your friend talk you into skiing?"

Steve shook his head. "I'm going to hang out at patrol headquarters for a while," he said. "Check out their new first-aid equipment. Then some of us are going to shoot some hoops down at the sports center."

For a second, Gregory was tempted by that idea. Shooting hoops with his uncle sounded like fun. And maybe a little safer than snowboarding with Tyler, Frogger, and Jason. But why come to a ski resort if all you're going to do is play basketball? He wasn't here to play it safe. If he couldn't be with his friends at home, he might as well have some adventures.

"Yo!" yelled Frogger from the lift line. "Gregory, right? Let's go!" He shifted over to let Gregory slide up next to him, one boot attached to his snowboard binding and the other pushing the board along.

The sun was shining and the snow was brilliant white. Every tree limb had a coating of frost that sparkled in the morning light. Gregory grinned as he slid onto the chairlift next to Frogger. This was going to be an awesome day!

"We're going to check out Jackrabbit," Frogger told Gregory, as the chairlift carried them up the hill. Tyler and Jason were in the chair right ahead of theirs.

Where was *that* trail? Gregory didn't remember the name. He pulled out his trail map.

Frogger snorted. "Don't bother, man," he said. "Most of the worthwhile trails aren't even *on* the map. If they are, the patrol just ropes them off so nobody but patrollers get to use them." He grinned. "Jackrabbit is *sick*. You'll love it. Just don't biff when you huck Little Rock."

Suddenly, Gregory's mouth felt dry. In his mind, he translated Frogger's words and realized that soon he'd be doing his best to follow this boy and his friends down a steep, narrow trail that wasn't even on the map. They'd all be jumping off some rock, and he'd probably be the only one to wipe out — or "biff," as Frogger put it.

Gregory licked his lips and managed a weak smile. "Sounds great, dude!" he said.

"Right!" yelled Patricia. "Now left! Snowboarder at ten o'clock!" She was having a blast, guiding Rachel on their third run down Bear Run, the widest, friendliest trail at North Woods. It was just perfect for warming up. Patricia felt good on her skis, considering that she hadn't been on them for about eleven months. It must have been all the ice hockey she'd been playing. Her legs were strong and she was in good shape. She took a few quicker turns to see how that felt, stopping short before she got too far ahead of Rachel. Yes! Skiing fast was *so* much fun.

"Coming to a trail merge," she told Rachel. "In a minute we'll be skiing on Bobcat, under the lift, and soon we'll be at the bottom." She checked up the hill to her right to make sure nobody was bombing down. So far, the coast looked clear. But what were those poles, higher up the hill on the other side of Upper Bobcat? She'd have to check it out as they rode up the lift.

"Looks like a racecourse," she reported to Rachel, a few minutes later as the chairlift zoomed them up the mountain. "There are red poles and blue ones. I think you're supposed to go around the red ones on your right, the blue ones on your left. Wow! That kid is going fast!"

When they got off at the top of the chairlift, Patricia saw a sign she hadn't noticed before. "'Citizen racing,'" she read out loud. "'One dollar a run. Proceeds benefit the Central Vermont Humane Society.'"

"You want to try it, don't you?" asked Rachel. "Go ahead. Didn't you tell me there's a bench up here? I'll take a break and wait until you come back up. The sun feels great." She turned her face toward the sun and smiled.

"Really?" Patricia asked. "Okay." She settled Rachel in on the bench and pushed off toward the racecourse, which was just a little way down Upper Bobcat. At the top of the course, a woman with a clipboard greeted her.

"Ready to race?" she asked.

Patricia nodded, pulling a crumpled dollar bill out of the pocket of her ski pants.

"The timer will start as soon as you make the first turn," the woman said. "You can get your results from the race monitor at the bottom."

Patricia looked down the racecourse. It looked a lot steeper from this angle. The poles didn't leave a lot of room for the kind of wide, graceful turns she'd been making on Bear Run. Patricia thought back to some ski racers she'd seen on TV. The idea was to ski aggressively, using the edges of your skis to carve strong, quick turns around the poles. She could do that. Right?

Patricia took a deep breath, bent her legs down into a squat, and pushed off.

"This is just like old times," Steve said, as he lounged in a ratty brown corduroy recliner. The arms were patched with duct tape and the headrest was leaking stuffing. "In fact, I think this chair was in the lounge back when I was patrolling! And it wasn't new then, either."

Ski patrol headquarters consisted of three rooms: an office, with the base radio, a phone, and file cabinets; the clinic area, which had three beds, a sink, and closets packed with first-aid supplies; and the lounge area, where there was a small kitchen plus tables, chairs, and lockers for the patrollers' gear.

Steve was visiting in the lounge, where patrollers hung out between accidents or when they were changing boots. Mr. Callahan had walked him over, along with the dogs, so that the patrollers could meet Santa Paws. After Mr. Callahan and the dogs had left, Steve had observed as the patrollers helped several injured skiers and snowboarders. His old friend Andy and a new patroller named AJ had just finished helping a boy with a sprained wrist.

Andy laughed. "Lotta naps get taken in that easy chair," he said. "When we're not out saving lives, that is." He reached down to tighten the buckles on his ski boots. "Sure you're not up for a few runs? It's pretty nice out there."

"Thanks, but I'll pass," said Steve. "Mark and AJ and I are going to shoot a few hoops before they sign in for the late shift."

"Sounds good," said Andy. "Just remember, I've got a hot new pair of skis and some boots that are just your size — you can borrow them anytime."

"Tempting," Steve said, adding *not* in his mind. He was on vacation, and he just wanted to relax.

* * *

"Do you think those are bobcat tracks?" asked Eileen Callahan, pointing to a set of footprints that crossed their trail and wound their way into a small cluster of fir trees. Each little tree was so heavily draped with snow that the firs looked like a gathering of snow gnomes, their pointy hats askew.

Eileen, Emily, and the two little girls had just passed the intersection of Maple Loop and Birch Run, which had been marked with a rustic wooden sign.

Emily checked her wildlife tracking book, paging through the pictures of animal signs. She shook her head. "Nope," she said. "More likely it's a rabbit — a snowshoe hare."

"Bunny!" yelled Miranda, stooping down to scoop up another handful of snow to lick. She *loved* snowshoeing. Poor Lucy had to get pulled in the sled, but Miranda was a big girl and got to walk on her very own snowshoes. The grown-ups weren't going fast at all — in fact, they stopped to look at every single footprint and tree — so it wasn't hard to keep up. The only thing that would be more fun would be if Cookie could come along. But dogs weren't supposed to go on the snowshoe trails because they might scare the wild animals that lived in the woods.

Not that they'd *seen* any wild animals. Or any tracks other than bunnies, bunnies, and more bunnies.

But the woods were beautiful, and the meandering path they followed ran along a frozen brook with swirling patterns in the ice.

Eileen sighed with pleasure. "Tom does not know what he's missing," she said, shaking her head.

Mr. Callahan did not feel as if he were missing a thing. In fact, at that moment his life could not have been more complete. His toes were toasty in his favorite Scooby-Doo slippers. There was a cup of hot chocolate and a plate full of cookies on the table next to the couch he lay on. The fire crackled, soft music — *Sinatra's Greatest Hits!* — filled the air, and the red fleece blanket covering him was soft and cozy. It was almost too much work to turn the pages of his book, but somehow he managed to find the energy.

Both dogs lay sprawled on the rug next to the couch, basking in the warmth radiating from the fireplace. Santa Paws sighed contentedly as he snuggled into a slightly more perfect position, adjusting his paws and tucking his tail beneath his chin. What could be better than this? The nice lady whose house this was had even brought him one of her wonderful dog biscuits when she delivered Mr. Callahan's cookies and cocoa. And, of course, she had given Cookie one of the fig squares off Tom's plate.

Life was good.

Then there was a sound.

It drowned out Frank's crooning.

It drowned out the crackling of the fire.

Santa Paws cocked an ear and looked up at Mr. Callahan. The man did not seem to hear what he was hearing. How could he miss that loud buzzing? It sounded like a giant bee, flying right outside. Or a whole bunch of bees. One buzzed by, and then another and another. Santa Paws got up and began to pace. Cookie leapt to her feet as well. Obviously, *she* heard the sound.

Both dogs had their ears up as they paced.

"Down, Santa Paws," mumbled Tom, around a mouthful of cookie. "Down, Cookie. We'll go out in a while. Right now, it's time to relax."

The dog paid no attention. In fact, he barely heard Mr. Callahan. He was concentrating on the noise outside.

Then, suddenly, his whole body tensed. He raised his head and pricked his ears as high as they could go. The hair on the back of his neck stood up.

He had heard a new sound. The sound of metal and wood, crashing and tangling. And then the buzzing stopped.

Santa Paws looked at Cookie. The black dog looked back, a worried expression on her alert face. Both of them knew that something was very, very wrong.

7

"What is it, Santa Paws?" Tom roused himself, sitting up on the couch and letting the red fleece blanket fall to the floor. "Cookie?"

Mr. Callahan had lived with Santa Paws long enough to know he should trust the dog's instincts. And now, with both dogs whining and pacing, there was no question in his mind.

Something was wrong.

Who was in trouble? Was it Gregory, out snowboarding? Patricia and Rachel, on their skis? What about his wife and Emily — and the two little girls? What if Steve had gotten into some sort of trouble? Mr. Callahan's mind was racing.

Santa Paws and Cookie were getting more frantic by the minute, tearing out into the hall and back again, whining and yelping.

"Okay, okay," said Mr. Callahan. "We'll go see what's up." He grabbed the sweater that was lying across the back of the couch and headed downstairs, Santa Paws and Cookie flying down in front of him. Nobody was in the main entrance. Tom guessed that Thea and Dan must both be out doing errands. He paused near the back door to kick off his slippers and pull on the boots he'd left there after walking the dogs that morning. Then he took his jacket off a hook and wound his blue knitted scarf — last year's Christmas gift from Patricia — around his neck. Where were his gloves and hat? He poked around on the shelves lining the small entrance that Thea called a mudroom.

Santa Paws couldn't stand it. What was taking so long? His heart was racing and he panted as he paced back and forth near the door. Cookie, who was just as agitated, jumped up again and again, paws on the door as if she could push it open.

Finally, Santa Paws began to bark. Cookie joined in, creating a chorus of alarm.

"Okay, forget the gloves," said Tom. "Just let me find your leashes. I can't let you run free in a strange place." He removed the brown leather leash from a hook and clipped it to Santa Paws's collar. Then he turned to look for Cookie's leash.

At that moment, Cookie's paw hit the doorknob, spinning it so that the door unlatched and opened toward her. Surprised, she stared for a moment at the widening crack between indoors and out. Then, without turning to look at Santa Paws, she squeezed through it and took off at full speed.

"Cookie!" yelled Tom. He ran to the door and

looked out. It was already starting to grow darker, but it was easy to see Cookie's black body against the white snow. She was heading straight for the place they had walked that very morning: the snowmobile trail. And she didn't slow down when she heard her name.

"Arrgh!" said Tom. "Well, what can we do? We'll have to follow her. But one loose dog is enough," he told Santa Paws. "You're sticking with me." He put his hand through the loop on the end of the leash. Then he and Santa Paws set out to follow Cookie.

It wasn't hard to find her. She was only a little way up the snowmobile trail, near the spot where it took a wide curve and headed uphill. She stood tensed, barking like mad at something lying on the side of the trail.

Tom picked up his pace, jogging along with Santa Paws straining at the leash. As he drew closer, he began to make out details. A black snowmobile lay on its side, just off the trail. Its front end was crumpled against a large maple tree. "But where's the rider?" Tom asked out loud. He began to run faster. By then, Cookie had stopped barking and had disappeared beyond the snowmobile.

Tom passed the steaming, broken hunk of metal machinery. His shoulder was on fire from the way Santa Paws was tugging at the leash.

"Oh, no!" he gasped, as soon as he could see.

A black-suited figure lay crumpled against another tree. Its position was unnatural: legs and arms were sprawled out onto the trail, the unfamiliar angles splayed awkwardly on the white snow.

And a stain of red was spreading from the person's head.

Cookie stood over the figure, silent now. She looked up at Mr. Callahan as if asking what to do.

Tom dropped the leash he was holding and fell to his knees beside the body. It was a man, he could see now. A young man, probably just a little older than Gregory. Blood gushed from a gash on his temple. He was not moving.

"Santa Paws!" said Tom. "Go get —"

But as he turned to look at his dog, he realized his order was unnecessary. Santa Paws was already flying back down the trail.

Tom bent down to touch the young man's shoulder. "Hey," he said. "Are you okay?" He watched to see if the man's chest rose and fell with breath. It did. But the only answer from the snowmobiler was a little moan. Tom put his fingers on the side of the man's neck, feeling for a pulse. Right away, he felt a pounding that told him the man's heart was beating fast.

Cookie stood nearby, completely calm now. She didn't bark or bounce. She just watched, waiting to see how she could help.

Tom reviewed the first-aid rules that he knew.

If the man was breathing and his heart was working, he did not need to do CPR. But that head wound was bleeding hard. He needed to stop it before the man lost too much blood and went into shock. He unwound the scarf from his neck and folded it up into a small square. Then he held it to the wound, hoping that the pressure would stop the flow of blood. He was careful not to move the snowmobiler's head, in case he had hurt his neck or back in the crash.

Tom sat back on his heels, still holding pressure against the wound. "Buddy," he said again. "Are you okay? Can you talk?"

Another tiny moan escaped the man's lips.

Next to Mr. Callahan, Cookie started to pace again. Ears up, she began to whimper. Tom turned to look at her. "What is it, Cookie?" he asked. He was not about to ignore her warning.

Cookie cocked an ear down the trail. It was that sound again, the buzzing. And it was coming closer. Mr. Callahan and this hurt man were in danger! She looked down the trail and barked. She barked again.

Tom looked up and listened, trying hard to hear what Cookie heard. Finally, it came to him. The whine of approaching engines! More snowmobilers were coming down the trail. With dusk falling quickly, they might not see the crash and the fallen driver in time. The injured man had to be moved — and fast!

It was important to pull him in a straight line, Tom knew. If he had hurt his back or neck, the injury could be made worse by moving him. But there was no choice. He had to get this man out of the trail. Letting go of the scarf for a moment, he went to the man's feet and began to tug, straightening out his legs. Once the legs were in a straight line, he began to pull harder, trying to move the man across the snow. It wasn't easy, since Tom was sinking into the softer snow on the side of the trail, all the way up to his knees.

Cookie seemed to sense that he needed help. Joining him at the injured man's feet, she grabbed hold of the fabric of his coveralls and began to tug, digging her feet into the snow. Since she was lighter, she didn't sink as far.

Her help made all the difference. Within seconds, the injured man was completely off the trail. And seconds after that, the roar of snowmobile engines grew louder, and a group of three raced past, hardly slowing as they took the turn. Their tracks raced right over the spot where the man had been lying only moments earlier.

Tom shook his head, amazed that they had not stopped to help. Then he heard the sound of their engines growing louder again as the snowmobilers turned around to come back.

Meanwhile, Santa Paws had raced up the snowmobile trail, back into the parking lot of the Winterhaus. He ran up the stairs and barked as loudly as he could. Nobody came to the door. He barked again, just to make sure nobody was there. Then he turned and began to run again. This time, he headed straight for the village at the bottom of the ski area. He had been there just this morning, and he knew there *had* to be help there.

He thought of the place Steve had taken him, with its familiar smells of bandages and antiseptic. That was it! It smelled just like the place near home with the trucks with flashing lights. The people there were always ready to help.

Santa Paws raced for the ski patrol headquarters. There it was, with the big white cross on its door! He ran onto its porch and began to bark at the closed door. A burly man came to see what the noise was all about. It was Andy, who recognized Santa Paws right away.

"Hey, it's that rescue dog that was here with Steve!" he said. "Maria, check it out!"

A tall blond woman wearing a red vest with a white cross on the front came to look. "He seems to want something," she said. "Hey, fella, what's up?"

"Maybe we should take him down to the sports center to find Steve," Andy said. "Steve'll know what he wants."

Moments later, a sweaty, red-faced Steve came to the door of the gym. "What's up?" he asked Andy.

"That dog," Andy said. "He's going nuts, barking and barking. We can't figure out what he wants."

Steve threw down the ball he was holding. "Santa Paws?" he asked. "He's here?" He grabbed his jacket from a row of hooks near the gym door and followed Andy outside. "What's up, buddy?" he asked the pacing, barking dog.

Minutes later, Steve, Andy, Mark, AJ, and a carload of first-aid equipment were heading down the road toward the Winterhaus. Maria had called for an ambulance, but there was no time to lose until it came. Santa Paws sat in the front seat, guiding the way by leaning against Steve when he wanted him to make a turn. Then, as soon the car doors opened in the B and B's parking lot, he dashed up the snowmobile trail, barking at Steve to follow, fast!

The patrollers ran behind him, carrying a backboard, a bag that held an oxygen tank, and their backpacks full of first-aid supplies.

"Thank goodness," said Tom, when he saw them coming. As they approached, an ambulance siren began to wail from the bottom of the resort's access road. "You're going to be all right, pal," he told the man lying in the snow. "Help is here."

8

"Oh, my!" said Grammy, as she speared a tomato from her salad plate.

Patricia loved it that she had a grandmother who actually said things like "Oh, my!" She smiled at Grammy across the table. "'Oh, my' is right!" she agreed. "That guy was totally lucky that Santa Paws and Cookie were around. His friends didn't even realize he wasn't behind them anymore. He could have been lying there for a long time."

"Or, more likely, he'd have been run over by the next snowmobiler," said Tom. "If Cookie hadn't heard that guy coming and helped pull him out of the trail —" IIe didn't finish his sentence. He didn't have to.

The Callahans were all together again, after a long day of going their separate ways. Over dinner with Grammy and Granddad at North Woods' best restaurant, Gretchen's Kitchen, they discussed the events of the day.

Mr. Callahan was on his fifth retelling of the snowmobile accident, and Steve was adding his part of the story. Grammy and Granddad made an excellent audience.

"Those dogs deserve a treat," said Granddad, slipping a huge hunk of his T-bone steak into a folded napkin.

Gregory and Patricia looked at each other across the table and smiled. Granddad loved to spoil the dogs. He never got over the way Santa Paws rescued people. Mr. and Mrs. Callahan had given up on telling him not to give the dogs so many treats.

Patricia nudged Rachel in the ribs, since she knew her friend couldn't see the smile. But instead of grinning at her and nudging her back, Rachel just rubbed the spot where Patricia had bumped her, an annoyed look on her face. What was *that* about, Patricia wondered.

"Well, our day was much quieter," she said, to change the subject. "Rachel and I just skied and skied, all day. It was a blast. I got faster on that racecourse every time I ran it!" Patricia could still feel the burn in the muscles of her legs, and the sensation of her skis whipping through those turns.

Rachel sat silently, scraping the last of her mashed potatoes — which Patricia had informed her were at three o'clock on her plate.

Suddenly, Patricia had the slightly uncomfortable feeling that she hadn't been quite fair to her friend. For every run she'd taken on the racecourse, Rachel had spent time on the bench at the top of the chairlift. She'd kept saying it was fine, that she was ready for a rest, that she enjoyed soaking up the sun. But now, Patricia realized that she'd only been being polite. She must have been bored stiff all day, waiting patiently while Patricia swooped down through the blue and red turns of the racecourse.

Patricia took another bite of her roast chicken, but it didn't taste nearly as savory as it had at first. She looked at Rachel again and felt a little knot in her stomach. She promised herself that she would make it up to her friend tomorrow. They would ski together all day long, and she would stay away from that racecourse, no matter what.

"Your day couldn't have been quieter than ours," reported Eileen. "I think the only sounds we heard all day were a woodpecker — and our own heavy breathing!"

"The woods were so lovely," agreed Emily. "There's something about the hush that comes over a place when it's all draped in snow. We really had time to look around and pay attention to what we saw."

"Did we tell you we spotted some coyote tracks?" Mrs. Callahan asked. "They cut right across the trail we were on. We think he was chasing a rabbit, because we saw rabbit tracks, too."

"There were bunny tracks all over!" chimed in Miranda. "I saw the tracks! But I didn't see one single bunny." She held up one finger, frowning.

"They're very well camouflaged, in their winter white," explained Mrs. Callahan. "But maybe tomorrow, if we're very, very quiet, we'll see one."

"You won't see as many tracks tomorrow, I'll bet," put in Steve, pointing out the window. The resort's lighted slopes were laid out in front of them. And the beam of each light showed millions of snowflakes pouring down from the sky.

It was snowing hard.

The snow had started while the patrollers and EMTs were carrying the snowmobiler, now strapped to a backboard, into the back of an ambulance. Santa Paws had looked up in surprise when a big white snowflake had landed on his nose. Before long, Cookie's curly coat was so covered in snow that she looked like a sheep that needed to be shorn.

The long hill of the access road was already covered in snow by the time the ambulance pulled out of the Winterhaus's parking lot. "The road could be greasy," Dan had told the driver. "But I saw the town snowplow go by a moment ago. Just take it slow and you'll be fine."

"Greasy?" asked Patricia, making a face.

"Slippery," Steve's friend Mark had translated. "This kind of wet, heavy snow can be tough to drive on. But these guys run their rig up and down our hill all the time. Just yesterday we had a guy who took a bad fall and dislocated his hip. They came up to get him."

The snow had continued as various Callahan family members arrived back at the Winterhaus, tired from their activities and ready to shower and change for dinner. Grammy and Granddad showed up only a little late — they were long-time Vermonters, and used to driving in snow. "My little Subaru can get us anywhere, anytime!" Grammy boasted.

"I wonder if my parents' Toyota will get them here," Rachel now wondered out loud, at dinner. "How much snow are we supposed to get, anyway? What if they don't make it for Christmas?" There was a slight quaver in her voice. Patricia reached out and touched her friend's hand.

"They'll make it," she said.

"What about Santa?" asked Miranda. "Mom and I left him a note so he would know where we are, but what if the snow is too deep and he can't make it?"

When she heard her older sister say the word "Santa," Lucy's eyes grew huge. "Santa!" she said. "Where's Santa?"

"He'll be here," said Emily soothingly. "Don't worry. After all, he knows that the day after tomorrow is special."

"It is?" asked Granddad, smiling broadly. "What day is it?" His eyes were dancing as he ticked off options on his fingers. "Can't be Arbor Day. You can't plant trees in the middle of winter. Not Halloween. The ghosts would freeze. The Fourth of July — well, obviously, that's in July, not December . . . "

Miranda couldn't take it anymore. "It's CHRIST-MAS!" she burst out.

Granddad looked shocked. "Christmas?" he asked. "What happens on Christmas?"

"Presents!" yelled Miranda.

As the other patrons in the restaurant turned to look, Emily reached out to put a hand on her daughter's shoulder. "Indoor voice, Miranda," she reminded her, with a smile. "Even at Christmas, we don't get to yell in restaurants."

"We'll have a bang-up Christmas," Granddad promised. "A little snow is nothing for Santa — or for us old-timers."

Steve looked over at Gregory. "You're awfully quiet tonight," he observed, raising his eyebrows at his nephew.

Gregory shrugged as he took another bite of his pork chop. "I'm beat," he said. "I spent the whole day snowboarding."

"Which trail was your favorite?" asked Steve.

Gregory shot him a look. "Um, probably Deer Path," he said. He nodded. "Yeah, Deer Path. I like that one."

In truth, he hadn't been on Deer Path all day. He remembered skiing down it — and liking its gentle curves — on other visits to North Woods. But his new friends laughed when he suggested taking a run on it. They never took *any* trail that was on the official trail map — unless it was roped off, that is. They ducked under every yellow rope they saw, after checking to make sure no patrollers were nearby to see them taking a closed trail. "Who wants to go where everybody *else* goes, man?" Frogger had asked.

Tyler had a nose for secret "lines" through the dense birch forests on the northern slopes of the mountain, an area the boys called Wilderness. These narrow, twisting trails had no official names, no signs to tell you how hard or easy they were. Not that any of them were easy!

"I call this one Mad Dog," said Tyler, leading the gang through a thicket of spruces toward a long, narrow snow-filled gully. "Some of the sweetest turns on the whole mountain are in here."

Gregory followed his new friends wherever they went. They swooped hollering through the trees as he bumbled along behind them, falling every few feet into the deep powder snow. It was a struggle to get up each time, and by the end of the day he was exhausted and bruised — but exhilarated. It had been one of the best, most exciting days of his life — even if he *had* come close to cracking his head on a tree on more than one occasion.

He looked over at his uncle across the dinner table. What would Uncle Steve think if Gregory said his favorite trail was Grizzly, or Werewolf? For all the years Steve had patrolled at North Woods, he probably didn't even know where those trails were.

"Did you hit any of the glades?" Steve asked just then, as if he were reading Gregory's mind. "Like Mousetrap?"

Gregory's eyes widened. Maybe his uncle *did* know about some of those trails. Mousetrap had been one of the steeper chutes Tyler had shown him that day. "Um — Mousetrap?" he asked, trying to look innocent. "Is that one of the trails off the gondola?"

Steve just grinned at him.

Gregory shrugged. "Maybe I was on it. Don't remember every trail."

"Just watch it," Steve warned. "Don't get in over your head. Remember, if one of the patrollers catches you on a closed trail, you can get your lift ticket yanked. Those trails are closed for a reason, usually because they're not safe to ski without more snow on them. And you shouldn't be cutting into lift lines, either."

Gregory blushed, thinking of the time he had followed Jason as he threaded his way through a long line of customers at the bottom of lift Two, pretending to look for his dad. They had hopped on the chairlift, laughing and slapping each other five as they looked back at the crowd.

"Gregory?" Mrs. Callahan asked. "You're not getting yourself into trouble out there, are you?"

"Mom!" he said. "I'm just snowboarding. Having a great time. Isn't that what you wanted when you guys decided we were all coming up here?" Gregory reached out for the little menu in the middle of the table. "So, what's for dessert?" he asked, changing the subject. "Yum, cheesecake. With strawberries. That's for me."

By the time they finished dinner, the Callahans' cars were covered in about five inches of fluffy powder. "It's really coming down!" said Mr. Callahan, as he brushed off the minivan's windshield. "Looks like we're going to have an extremely white Christmas!"

9

"Yesss!" Gregory stared out the window, grinning like a fool. He had jumped out of bed as soon as he woke up. There was a special hush in the air, and light was bouncing off the walls in his room, making it even brighter than it had been the morning before. Two clues that added up to . . . lots and lots of snow. Gregory had dashed to the window and pulled the curtains open, nearly tripping over Santa Paws in his rush to see how much they'd gotten. Six inches? A foot?

Over two feet of fluffy white snow festooned the deck outside the sliding glass doors. And it was all new. Gregory knew that for sure, because Dan had shoveled the deck the afternoon before.

Plus, snow was still falling. Gregory craned his neck to look up past the B and B's roofline. Fat flakes twirled down out of a windless white sky.

"Check it out, big guy!" Gregory said to Santa Paws, who had joined him by the window. The

87

dog stretched, then gave himself a hearty wake-up shake, making his collar tags dance and jingle. "This is what winter is all about. Vermont rules!"

Santa Paws yawned. Then, deciding that breakfast wasn't in the immediate picture, he went back to curl up on his bed for a few more minutes of delicious sleep. It was good that Gregory was happy, but the dog couldn't really see what all the excitement was about. All that snow just made it harder to run. It took all *kinds* of extra energy to bound through drifts like that. No, Mr. Callahan had the right idea: stay inside by the fire and relax.

Gregory didn't even want to take time for breakfast. But when his uncle Steve reminded him that the lifts didn't start up until nine o'clock, he decided that the pecan waffles Thea was serving might be worth sitting down for, after all.

"Is this real maple syrup?" Eileen asked, savoring a bite of waffle she had swirled into the sweet brown puddle on her plate.

"Of course!" said Thea, smiling as she refilled Tom's coffee cup. "Our neighbor makes it. He still gathers all his sap with horse-drawn sleds. You should come up at sugaring time and help out! It's hard work but lots of fun."

"Hard work? Fun?" said Tom. "I'm not sure I would use those two words in the same sentence." He had his book and reading glasses on the table next to him and his Scooby slippers were on his feet. He was all set to head for the couch right after breakfast.

"Patrolling was hard work sometimes," Steve mused. "But we always had fun. On days like this, we would get first tracks as we checked the trails to see which ones were safe for customers. There's nothing quite like skiing in powder like this." He gazed out the window, looking a little wistful.

"Well, why don't you?" asked Emily. "Andy said he had equipment to lend you, didn't he? You should go out with those guys, just for old times' sake."

"You know what?" said Steve suddenly. "I think I will. These conditions are just too good to pass up. So what if I haven't skied in years? I'll just take it easy, that's all."

"Go, Uncle Steve!" said Gregory, reaching out a fist to bump against his uncle's. "Rip it up!"

Steve smiled. "I *said* I'm going to take it easy."

"Me, too," said Patricia. "No more racing today. I'm just going to enjoy cruising down Bear Run. How does that sound, Rachel?"

"Really?" Rachel looked a little surprised. "That sounds great!" She smiled at her friend.

"And maybe we'll *see* a bear while we're out snowshoeing," said Eileen. "Who knows what animals might be running around out there in this storm?"

"Not these two, I can guarantee that," said Tom, looking down at Cookie and Santa Paws. "I'll take them out for a walk on the snowmobile trail, but after wading through all that snow, I'm guessing they'll be very happy to do the smart thing and cozy up by the fire with me."

Eileen shook her head. "You're missing a whole beautiful world out there," she told her husband.

"I trust you to tell me all about it, my dear," he answered happily, helping himself to another strip of bacon.

An hour later, Steve was in patrol headquarters buckling the boots Andy had lent him. "This feels like old times," he said to Mark, who was also booting up for the day. "Remember that blizzard in March of — what was it, eighty-seven?"

"Eighty-eight," Mark said. "I'll never forget it. We skied like crazy all day, then crashed in here on the cots and skied all day the next day, too. And the best part was that we didn't have one single injury that weekend. Nobody so much as sprained a finger."

"Let's hope today is like that, too," said Steve. "I keep up on my first-aid skills, but I don't want anyone getting hurt today — including myself!" He pulled up the suspenders on his ski pants, shrugged into his jacket, and buckled the chin-strap on the helmet he had borrowed from Maria.

"Ready?" asked Mark.

"Ready as I'll ever be," said Steve. They headed outside and shouldered their skis, ready to hike through the growing drifts to the bottom of the chairlift.

Mark spoke into his radio. "Mark to the top of Lift Two," he said, calling the patrollers who were on duty in the patrol shack at the top of the mountain. "I'm on my way up, with a special guest."

Meanwhile, Patricia and Rachel had already taken one run on Bear Run and were riding the chairlift back up the mountain.

"It feels funny to have the snowflakes flying against my cheeks," said Rachel. "I bet it's hard to see, with all that snow in the air."

"A little," Patricia said. "My goggles help." She looked down from the lift at the racecourse. The poles were almost half buried in snow, but it was still easy to see them. She wondered what it would be like to ski the course in all that powder. It would be slower but probably fun in a whole different way. It didn't look as if anyone had skied the course yet that day. Were they collecting a fee? Or would it just be free today, because of all the snow? She strained her eyes as the chairlift carried her past the course, trying to make out through the flying snow if anyone was standing in the starting shack.

"Patricia!" Rachel said suddenly. "Aren't we near the top? It seems as if we've been riding for a long time."

Patricia turned to look ahead. "Yikes!" she said. "You're right!" Quickly, she raised the safety bar — just in time. "Skiing off now," she told Rachel. Her friend held Patricia's elbow lightly as they skied off the chair.

She felt a rush of relief as they glided to a stop near the top of Bobcat and paused to put their hands back through the wrist straps on their ski poles. If Rachel hadn't spoken up, she might not have been able to raise the safety bar in time and they'd have ridden the chair around the big wheel at the top of the lift — Uncle Steve said it was called a bullwheel — and all the way back down the mountain. How embarrassing would *that* have been?

"Listen, Rach —" she said. She was still thinking about that racecourse, half buried in powder. "I just have to try one run on the racecourse. I'm dying to find out what it's like to make those turns in this deep snow." She paused, biting her lip. "You understand, don't you?"

Rachel hesitated. "Sure," she said, after a moment. "Go ahead."

"Really?" asked Patricia. "Okay. Are you going to wait up here?"

"No," said Rachel. "I think I know Bear Run pretty well by now. And I bet I can find someone to help guide me. I'll meet you at the bottom." She adjusted her orange vest. "You can still see me, even with all the snow coming down, right?"

"Definitely," said Patricia. "Nobody's going to run into you. Okay, meet you at the bottom!" Before she could change her mind, she pushed off down the slope, heading for the racecourse.

"Steve was right," said Emily. "There aren't too many tracks out here today. Or at least they're getting covered up before we can really see them."

"But it's so beautiful I don't even care," said Mrs. Callahan. "Do you?"

"Not at all," answered Emily. "Having fun, girls?" She looked down at her daughters. Miranda was clomping along happily in her snowshoes, raising her face now and then to stick out her tongue and catch snowflakes to swallow. Lucy seemed content in her sled. She was all zipped up in her pink snowsuit, and only her eyes showed. They were wide open, taking in the still, quiet woods around her.

"I think the snow is slowing down a bit," said Emily. "Look, here's a track that's still kind of fresh. What do you suppose made that? It's awfully deep. It must have been made by a pretty heavy animal." She stopped to take off her backpack and rummage for her tracking book. "Drat," she said. "I must have left it on the table this morning."

"Let's follow the track," suggested Mrs. Callahan. "Maybe we can put together some clues and figure out what kind of animal it was."

"Why not?" asked Emily. "That's the beauty of snowshoes. We don't have to stay on a trail. We can go wherever we want." She put her backpack back on. "Lead on, mystery animal!" she said.

Gregory wouldn't have noticed *dinosaur* tracks where he was. He was going way too fast for that, and having way too much fun to slow down. So far, he and his friends Jason, Tyler, and Frogger had managed to check out four of their favorite Wilderness trails. The deep powder made the steep parts a little less scary, since it slowed things down a bit and cushioned his falls. Or was Gregory just getting used to the wild trails his friends preferred? He could tell that his snowboarding had improved a *ton* already because of the way he was pushing himself.

"Okay," Frogger said, when the four boys had stopped, panting a bit, in the middle of the trail he called Boa Constrictor. "Here's the plan. We'll do one more run, like on Grizzly maybe, then break for lunch. After that, it's time to head for the Zoo."

"The Zoo?" asked Gregory. That name was new to him.

"Sure," said Frogger. "Gotta hit the Zoo today. It's too steep to ride in there unless there's this much powder. But it'll rock today!"

"How do we get there?" asked Gregory.

"Easy," Jason said. "We take the gondola all the way to the top. Then we hike up the ridgeline a ways. We drop in just above that ravine you can see to your right when you're riding up the lift."

Gregory felt his heart skip a beat. Was he really ready for the Zoo? Did he have to push himself that much? After all, he was having a great time already. Maybe he should just stick with the exciting new trails he'd already been introduced to.

Tyler looked at him, peering through the falling snow. "You in, man?" he asked.

Gregory paused.

"You can't miss this," Frogger said. "Nobody but locals like us knows where the Zoo is. You'd never find it on your own."

Gregory thought about telling his friends back in Oceanport about boarding in the Zoo. "Yeah," he'd say. "Cool trail. It's a total secret, though. Only locals know about it."

He looked back at Frogger, blinking away a snowflake that stuck to his eyelash. "I'm in," he said.

Tom Callahan was enjoying the feeling of the hot, tropical sun on his face. The sound of the waves lapping on shore was so soothing. Perhaps later he'd go snorkeling — or would it be more relaxing to just walk down the beach, searching for shells?

But — what was that sound? Was it a seal, barking like a dog? No, there were no seals in the Carribean. Perhaps it was a seagull. Tom tried to relax again — but someone was tugging at his beach towel. "Hey," he said, trying to grab it back. "What are you doing? I'm trying to relax here."

The tugging didn't stop. Nor did the seagull calls.

Finally, Tom opened his eyes. He wasn't on a beach at all! He was in a cozy room, with a crackling fire.

And there were two dogs in the room with him. Santa Paws was pulling at the red blanket over Tom's legs. Cookie was barking. As soon as she saw his eyes open, Cookie stuck her face into Tom's and gave him a big, sloppy kiss.

10

"Nice, Cookie," said Tom, drowsily. "From tropical breezes to dog breath, in one easy step. You sure know how to wake somebody from a wonderful dream."

Cookie kissed him again. Then she began to bark. And bark.

"Cookie, hush!" said Tom. "I mean, speak! I mean, don't speak!" He remembered that Patricia had taught Cookie to bark on command. When Patricia said, "Speak," Cookie would bark. So when you said, "Don't speak!" she was supposed to *stop* barking.

Cookie knew what it meant. But she was not about to stop. She and Santa Paws both knew that something was very, very wrong — and that it was up to them to try to make things right. She barked some more — short, sharp *woofs*, very different from the bark she used to scare away the boy who came to their porch every day with the newspaper, or the happy bark she used when she heard Miranda's voice in another room, or the "play with me" bark she bothered Santa Paws with when he wasn't in the mood for games.

"Come on, Cookie," mumbled Tom, yawning. He couldn't seem to wake up and leave that tropical dream behind. "You're going to get us kicked out of this nice, cozy place. Do you want to spend the rest of our vacation camping in the snow?"

Santa Paws had been pacing up and down, whining a little, while Cookie barked at Mr. Callahan. Now he came over to join his furry black friend, sitting himself right down in front of Mr. Callahan and joining Cookie in her barking.

Tom put his hands over his ears. "All right, already!" he cried. "I can't take it anymore!" He threw off his blanket and stood up, sighing and rubbing his back. This routine of the dogs seemed familiar — but there couldn't be another injured snowmobiler. This time, they were just being pesty. He was sure of it.

Cookie spun around in circles, barking even more loudly. Santa Paws rushed to the door and back again three times by the time Mr. Callahan had finished putting on his slippers.

With the dogs leading the way, Tom went down the stairs to the back door. "Wonder if I need my hat," he said, opening the door a crack to see how cold it was outside. This time he would be more careful about letting the dogs escape.

Cookie thrust her nose into the tiny opening and pushed — hard.

"Hey!" shouted Mr. Callahan, as Cookie flew outside. Santa Paws pushed past him, too, and the two dogs took off at a gallop up the snowmobile trail — in the direction of the snowshoe trails. "Santa Paws!" yelled Mr. Callahan. "Cookie! Wait!"

But the dogs, silent now, had already disappeared around a corner.

Mr. Callahan felt a chill go up his spine. Suddenly, he was wide awake. "Why didn't I figure it out before?" he asked himself. "Something *is* wrong. Somebody's in trouble." He gazed up the snowmobile trail, thinking of his wife and Emily and his two little nieces, out in an unfamiliar forest on their snowshoes. Even though it was only early afternoon, the blank white sky that had hung so low all day was beginning to darken. The snow was still falling. And it was only going to get colder as night came on. Mr. Callahan thought for a second about what to do. Then he turned to grab his jacket and pull on his boots.

"Are we lost, Mommy?" Miranda tugged on Emily's jacket sleeve.

"Lost? No, honey, of course not," Emily said.

Then she glanced up at her sister-in-law with a questioning look.

Eileen chimed in quickly. "Lost? No way! We're just having a nice ramble in the woods. We'll come out soon, right near our own little bed and breakfast. I wonder what kind of cookies Thea made today."

"Chocolate chip, I hope!" Miranda said. "Or maybe peanut butter, so Cookie can have one. She'd like that." Miranda trudged along for a few more steps, following Emily's trail. "Mommy?" she asked again, after a moment. "I miss Cookie. When will we be back?"

Emily shot another look at Eileen. "Soon, honey," she said. "Any minute." Then she bent to check on Lucy. "Are you warm enough, snuggle-bug?" she asked, adjusting the fleece-trimmed hood on Lucy's snowsuit.

Lucy's cheeks were pink but warm. Her snow-suit was dusted with snowflakes. She smiled up at her mother. "I *love* snow," she said, opening her arms wide.

"So do I, honey," said Emily, gazing up at the flakes drifting down. The snow had not stopped falling all day. They must have picked up at least another six inches since morning.

"You know," said Eileen, in a determinedly cheerful tone, "I think it might be fun to follow our own trail back home! You know, just turn around and follow our tracks." She gave Emily a significant look, eyebrows raised.

Emily knew exactly what that meant. It meant, "Don't scare the girls, but I think we may be a little bit lost after all."

"But I thought we were almost home!" Miranda wailed. "I don't *want* to go all the way back." She sank down until she was sprawled in the snow. "I'm tired."

"And if you sit there in the snow, you'll be cold, too," Emily said briskly. "Come on, sweetie, let's keep moving. We'll be back by the fireplace before you know it. And you can have *two* cookies, even if it *is* almost dinner time." She pushed up her jacket sleeve to check her watch. Then she turned to Mrs. Callahan. "Three o'clock," she mouthed, over Miranda's head.

Eileen remembered that the sun had been going down at about four-thirty lately. That didn't give them much time to find their way back to the warmth and coziness of the Winterhaus.

"I can almost taste one of Thea's yummy cookies," said Eileen. "Let's get going!" She started off, following the tracks they'd just made through an open glade of white birches.

Emily and the girls followed behind. For fifteen minutes or so, nobody spoke. Eileen had set a brisk pace, and it took all their energy to step through the soft, deep drifts.

Soon, though, Eileen slowed down. Their trail had wound down and around through a thick spruce forest. If she remembered right, they should be emerging soon into a stand of older maples. But the trail was getting harder to see, as snow continued to fall and fill in their tracks. The light was fading, too. Eileen bent down to get a closer look at the ground in front of her. Then she straightened up, ready to turn around and call out to Emily to come help her find the trail.

Instead, her mouth opened and shut again without a single sound emerging. She stared straight ahead toward a small clump of trees. What was that huge, dark shadow that seemed to be moving toward them through the falling snow?

She squinted into the growing darkness. Was it a rescuer, coming to find them?

The shadow loomed larger as it continued toward her. Suddenly, it took form. She saw a huge, broad flank. Long, spindly legs with knobby knees. And a gigantic head, shaped sort of like a horse's.

It was a moose.

It was the size of a Volkswagen Bug.

And it was coming straight toward her.

Santa Paws leapt through the snowdrifts, diving like a dolphin as he pushed off again and again with his powerful hind legs. His front paws churned through the light, soft powder as if it were water and he was doing the dog paddle. Moving through snow this deep took even more energy than fighting the waves in a stormy ocean, which he had done more than once to save a drowning person.

His mind was clear and sharp; the cold air had chased away all the laziness of a day spent in front of the fire. His nose twitched as he raised it to the wind, sniffing for the faint scents that mixed with the snowflakes swirling around his head. He smelled his people. Mrs. Callahan, Emily, the two little ones. They were out here — and they were frightened. He galloped on, moving as if in slow motion through the deep snow.

Behind him, Cookie leapt and dove as well. Though her legs were shorter, her springy muscles and light build served her well as she made her way through the drifts. It didn't hurt that Santa Paws had broken trail ahead of her, either. Cookie's eyes, usually twinkly and mischievous, were focused like laser beams on the form of Santa Paws just ahead. She held her nose high, constantly sniffing and reading the scents that drifted through the cold, snow-filled air. There were several that were familiar, but one of them set her heart racing and gave her muscles a boost that sent her flying through the snow. Miranda!

Then another scent, rank and powerful, mixed with the familiar odors. The hair stood up on the back of both dogs' necks when they smelled it.

Animal.

Big animal.

Wild animal.

"Moose," said Eileen, only no sound came out when she spoke. She licked her lips and tried again. "Moose!" she said. Her eyes were fastened on the huge animal that loomed larger and larger as it approached. It was moving slowly, but in a straight line — straight toward her and her family.

Behind her, she heard Emily gasp.

"What *is* that, Mommy?" Miranda cried. "Is it a horse? Why is a horse in the woods?"

Eileen tore her eyes away from the approaching moose and turned to meet Emily's eyes. "Run! Get behind a tree," she ordered. "Take Lucy. I'll take Miranda." She reached out to grab Miranda's hand. "Come with me, honey," she said, pulling her three steps to the left before Miranda could object. Three steps away from the moose. Three steps that took them behind a spruce tree.

A small spruce tree.

Not *nearly* big enough to hide behind. Not nearly big enough to stop an animal the size of Rhode Island from trampling them into the snow.

Emily and Lucy cowered behind another spruce nearby.

"What does it want?" Emily whispered.

"I don't know," Eileen answered in a low voice. "It's not as if it wants to hurt us. Moose are herbivores, I know that much. They eat grasses and things." She thought for a second. "I remember the wildlife book said that they have terrible vision. Maybe it's just trying to figure out what we are."

"Well, it's trying pretty hard," said Emily, in a choked voice.

Eileen followed her gaze and saw that the moose had not stopped coming toward them. It was only an arm's length away, and it seemed bigger than ever. She had to crane her neck to take in its whole height, and its massive form nearly filled her field of vision. It swung its huge, heavy head back and forth, up and down, snorting a little. The animal was so close now that Eileen could smell its rank, wild odor. She felt puffs of its breath on her cheek.

"Help!" she yelled, without thinking. "Help! Help!"

Santa Paws froze. His ears pricked forward. Was it the wind? No, it was a voice. A voice he knew well. He stood stock-still, listening as hard as he could. Behind him, Cookie cocked her head. Then the two dogs plunged back into the drifts, running faster and harder than ever.

11

Santa Paws burst into the spruce grove, barking at the top of his lungs. Cookie was right next to him. Her higher-pitched bark blended with his to create a frantic duet.

Eileen let go of the tree trunk she was gripping and sank to her knees in the snow. What a relief! She felt like crying. Santa Paws and Cookie had found them. Now they were safe.

But in the next moment, all her fears flooded back. What if the moose charged at the dogs? Brave and strong as he was, Santa Paws wouldn't have a chance. The moose would flatten him instantly. And Cookie? Eileen looked down at Miranda. The little girl must be kept from seeing the dog she adored get hurt, if it came to that.

Emily's eyes met her sister-in-law's. Both women were thinking the same thing. Emily bent to whisper something to Lucy, and Eileen turned back to look at the moose.

It had turned partway around, and it was now staring at the two barking dogs. It was still swinging its head from side to side, then nodding and pawing the ground, then swinging its head again. It took a step toward Santa Paws and Cookie, then another.

Eileen drew in a breath. "Santa Paws," she said, almost in a whisper. "Don't be a hero. Take care of yourself." She realized that it was no use, even as she said the words. If necessary, the dog would die for her, and she knew it.

Santa Paws felt the gaze of the big, wild animal. He met it head-on, staring back with blazing eyes. Part of him wanted to bolt, to turn tail and run as fast and as far as he could through the drifting snow, through the trees, through the growing darkness.

But that was only a tiny part. The rest of him knew he must stand up to this beast, chase it off, keep his people safe.

Cookie could see past the animal to Miranda, cowering next to Mrs. Callahan. How *dare* this animal frighten her so badly! Cookie barked louder, and took three dancing steps forward.

The moose reared up its head, rolling its big eyes back so far that the whites showed.

Santa Paws sensed that the animal was afraid. He, too, took a few steps forward, baring his teeth as he barked his most vicious, growling bark.

The moose tossed its head again. It picked up one of its feet, its strange, spindly leg seemingly bending backward at the knee. Then another foot, and another. It turned, as slowly as an ocean liner, and moved silently off toward an opening in the spruces.

Santa Paws and Cookie followed the moose, barking and nipping at its heels. Instinctively, they knew that once the animal had turned, it wanted to get away and would not turn again and strike out at them.

Once the moose had traveled beyond the circle of spruces, Cookie dropped back and plunged through the drifts, straight to Miranda's side. The little girl was standing stock-still, not yet sure it was all right to relax. Cookie snuggled up against her and stretched her nose up to touch Miranda's cheek.

"Good girl, Cookie," said Eileen, reaching down to stroke the dog's curly coat. "What a good girl you are."

At that, Miranda burst out crying and flung her arms around Cookie. "You saved us!" she wailed.

Eileen saw Santa Paws trot back into the clearing. She turned to Emily. "I think we're safe now," she said.

Emily grimaced. "Great," she said. "I mean, really, that's great. There's only one problem." She was sitting on the snow, and now she struggled to get up. "I think I twisted my ankle when I ran over here." She bit her lip as she tried to stand. "Ouch!" She collapsed again into the snow.

"Mommy?" Lucy asked.

"Mommy has a boo-boo," Emily told her daughter. She looked helplessly at Eileen. "Now what? It's getting dark."

Sure enough, it was suddenly harder for the two women to see each other, even though they were only a few feet apart.

"I'll help you," said Eileen. "You can lean on my shoulder. We can make it." She tried to keep the rising panic out of her voice. The girls would be terrified if they knew how bad the situation really was. It was cold. The snow was still falling. Their tracks were covered. It was growing dark. There was a moose lurking somewhere nearby. They had only a few PowerBars and a small bottle of water, and no camping gear, flashlight, or any other survival equipment.

Trouble. They were in big trouble, and Eileen knew it. She kneaded her hands together, thinking.

Santa Paws looked up at her. He sensed her anxiety. He reached up and pawed gently at her arm, whining.

"Can you help, Santa Paws?" Mrs. Callahan looked down at him. "Can you help us find the way home?"

Santa Paws whined again.

"Maybe we shouldn't move," Emily suggested. "Aren't you supposed to stop moving when you're lost, and let people find you? Maybe we should huddle together to stay warm, and wait for rescue."

As if she understood what Emily was saying, Cookie moved in closer to Miranda, pressing her whole body against the girl's slight frame.

"You know," said Eileen, "that's probably not a bad idea. We can tear down some of these spruce boughs and build a little roof over our heads to keep the snow off. It'll be just like playing house." She tried to make it sound like fun, for Miranda's sake.

She looked down at the dog sitting next to her. "Santa Paws," she said. "Get help. Go get help."

Santa Paws knew what that meant. He had done it so many times before. He would run to a neighbor's house, or to the place where the people in uniforms kept their first-aid equipment and the special trucks with the sirens and lights. But here, in the woods, things were different. Where was help now? Then he remembered the place he had gone the day before, the place where Steve's friends worked.

He looked at Cookie. Now she was curled between Miranda and Lucy, keeping the children as warm as she could. She gazed back at him without moving a muscle. Her meaning was clear. She would stay there, in the spruce grove. He must go find help.

Santa Paws barked once, then turned and ran off into the gathering gloom. Eileen's heart sank as she watched him disappear. She'd felt so much safer with him by her side. But, she told herself, he had always been able to help before. Why would this time be any different?

Back on the mountain, Patricia lay between two blue bamboo poles, tears rolling down her face. Once again, she had gotten pulled into the fun of running the racecourse, and she hadn't been able to stop with one run. Rachel had seemed okay skiing alone — or so Patricia had told herself. In fact, she was probably at the bottom of the hill right now, waiting to ride up the chairlift with Patricia.

But Patricia was not going to be showing up anytime soon. Not with the way she'd hurt her knee. The snow, so deep and soft, was suddenly the enemy. Her ski tip had buried itself in a drift as she came hard around the last turn. She had fallen backward and her leg had twisted awkwardly. Her ski bindings had finally released when she landed, but it was too late. Now her knee hurt so badly she couldn't even *think* about getting up and putting her skis back on.

She lay there, wondering what to do. Should

she call out to one of the people riding by on the chairlift? She felt like a fool. The lights for night skiing had come on, even though it wasn't really dark yet. Maybe if she could just untangle herself and get up, she could walk down the mountain, carrying her skis. If she stayed over on the side of the slope where the lights didn't reach, nobody would know what an idiot she had been.

Then she heard the sound of skis swishing through the powder above her. Oh, no! Was somebody bombing through the racecourse? Was she about to become roadkill?

"Hey, there," said a friendly female voice. "What happened to you?"

Patricia looked up and saw a blond woman in a red jacket. Ski patrol. Great. She was really going to hear it from Uncle Steve now. "Nothing. I just fell," she said.

"So we figured," said the patroller, who had already stepped out of her skis and arranged them in a big X uphill, to warn off other approaching skiers. "I'm Maria — and you must be Steve's niece Patricia. Your friend Rachel was worried about you when you didn't turn up at the bottom, and she told us where you were skiing. What hurts?"

Patricia pointed to her knee.

"Hmm," said Maria, squatting down to take a closer look. "Did you hear any kind of sound when you fell?"

"I might have heard a little pop," Patricia admitted.

"And did you hurt anything else? Your back? Your neck?"

Patricia shook her head.

After a few more questions and a little bit of poking and prodding, Maria spoke into the radio in her chest pocket. "Maria to ski patrol base. I'm going to need a toboggan and a Sun Valley splint on the racecourse, about three quarters of the way down Upper Bobcat." She turned to Patricia and smiled. "Ready to go for a ride?"

Santa Paws had not gone far when he heard the sound of approaching voices. He veered toward them.

"Hey!" yelled a man, when he saw the dog bound toward them. "It's that dog! Santa Paws. We must be getting close."

Mr. Callahan had gone straight to the ski patrol base when the dogs had run off. Within fifteen minutes, a search party had been organized. Five patrollers had grabbed backpacks full of extra warm clothes and blankets. They had flashlights, whistles, extra food and water, first-aid equipment, and even sleeping bags and tents, in case they had to stay out longer than they expected.

The search party had been hiking for a half hour already, following the faint trail that was already being covered by new-fallen snow. The sight of Santa Paws confirmed that they were on the right track.

"I bet he already found them," said a patroller named Hal. "Look at the way he keeps running back and forth, showing us the trail he was using. He wants us to go that direction."

Santa Paws ran back up the trail one more time, and the rescuers followed him. As the rescuers picked up his tracks and moved toward Mrs. Callahan, Emily, and the two children, Santa Paws turned back toward the ski area and stood still, as if listening. His nose quivered. His ears were pricked.

Trouble.

He had no time to waste.

He knew Mrs. Callahan and the others would be safe now — but someone else was not. Without a backward glance, he took off running as fast as he could, using the track that the rescuers had stomped down with their snowshoes.

"Rachel, I am *so* sorry," Patricia said. She was lying on one of the beds in the clinic area of patrol headquarters, with a splint on her leg and a bag of snow icing her hurt knee. "I messed up. I am the worst friend ever, and you are the best. You saved me, even though I left you to ski alone all day!"

Rachel shrugged. "What was I going to do,

leave you for the vultures?" she asked with a smile.

The boy sitting next to her laughed appreciatively. "You are *so* funny," he said, running a hand through his wavy brown hair.

And you are so cute! Patricia thought, taking in his smile. It figured that Rachel had met — and impressed — a guy like this Robert. He'd helped guide her down Bear Run a few times and he was obviously completely smitten. Patricia looked wryly down at her knee. It served her right. She had a bum knee, and Rachel had a new boyfriend.

Maria sat nearby, filling out an accident report. Steve and Mr. Callahan hovered near the headquarters radio, listening to the reports from the patrollers who had found Mrs. Callahan, Emily, and the girls. All four were fine — with the exception of Emily's ankle — and on their way back. Three patrollers were pulling Emily in Lucy's sled, while a fourth carried Lucy piggyback.

"It's almost time for the torchlight parade," said Maria, checking her watch. She helped Patricia sit up. "If you look out the window, you'll see all the patrollers skiing down the mountain in a line, carrying flares. It's a Christmas Eve tradition here at North Woods."

"And you don't get to be in it, because of me," Patricia said.

"That's okay," Maria said. "My feet were getting cold, anyway. I was due for a warm-up break." She pulled the curtains open and turned down the inside lights so everyone could see outside.

Suddenly, there was a scratching at the door.

Steve went and threw it open. "Santa Paws!" he said. "My man! Great to see you."

Santa Paws limped into patrol headquarters, his coat full of snow. Balls of ice had begun to form between the pads of his feet, and he was thirsty and hungry and exhausted. He sat on the doormat and began to bite at the ice balls, which pulled at the hairs between his pads and hurt his sensitive feet. He'd bite for a minute, then get up and pace and whine. He could not seem to settle down.

"Poor buddy," said Steve, rubbing the dog's ears. "You're beat. But now you can relax and watch the torchlight parade with us. Everybody's safe."

"Wait," said Patricia. "Where's Gregory?"

12

"Help!"

Gregory couldn't believe how weak his voice sounded. He could barely hear *himself*, for Pete's sake. How was anybody else going to hear him? Not that there was anybody nearby. He was out in the middle of nowhere, all by himself, stuck upside down in the soft, loose snow around the trunk of a small spruce. His snowboard was tangled in the tree's lower branches. Snow was all around his face, and every time he moved, it packed in tighter. Soon he wouldn't be able to breathe at all. And there was no escape. He couldn't get his snowboard off. The snow was so soft and fluffy that there was nothing to push against, even if he *could* untangle his legs from the tree branches.

What a stupid way to die, thought Gregory.

He should have known better. The whole idea of boarding in the Zoo had frightened him a little, but he had been too embarrassed to bail out of the plan. His new friends would have thought he was a baby! They probably wouldn't even have tried to change his mind if he'd said he wasn't coming — they'd have just shrugged and taken off without him.

Some friends.

It was still plenty light out when the four boys had gotten off the gondola and carried their snowboards over to a roped-off trail that led even farther up the mountain. HIKING TRAIL read a sign posted near the rope. NOT FOR WINTER USE. But Frogger pointed out footprints in the snow. "Everybody goes here," he said.

"Isn't it a little late to start heading into the woods?" Gregory asked, looking up at the sky. The sun was nothing but a small white disk, barely peeking out through the thick, low clouds that were still dropping fat snowflakes.

"Nah," said Jason. "It's only about a ten-minute hike. Then we drop in, and it's, like, thirty seconds down! It's wicked steep in there." He grinned maniacally and smacked fists with Frogger.

"It's a tradition," Tyler told him. "On powder days we always make the Zoo our last run."

"Let's move," said Frogger, looking back over his shoulder. "Red coat at ten o'clock."

Gregory followed his gaze and saw a patroller coming out of the building at the top of the gondola. Was it one of Uncle Steve's friends? He squinted, trying to make out the person's face. But the flying snow made it hard to see anything. Anyway, the person seemed to be facing the other way.

Tyler ducked under the bright yellow rope, holding it up for the others. He smiled at Gregory. "You'll love it," he said. "The Zoo is worth the trip."

Gregory swallowed hard. "Can't wait," he lied.

Frogger led the way along the narrow, twisting trail. It ran across the mountain, and a little uphill, through a thicket of spruce trees. The others followed, carrying their snowboards. Every step was a challenge, since the snow was so deep. Even though other people had passed that way, the trail was hardly what you'd call packed. Gregory floundered along, sweating and breathing hard. Every few steps, he would sink in almost up to his hips. He had never seen such deep snow before — even in the White Mountains.

At one point when Gregory stopped to catch his breath, he also checked his watch. The ten-minute hike had already taken over half an hour! The sky — at least the part of it he could see between the tree branches — was beginning to grow a little dim.

Finally, Frogger came to a stop. "Awesome," he said, looking downhill. "Only a few tracks so far."

Gregory caught up and looked down the trail. "Man," he said, under his breath.

Frogger grinned at him. "Cool, huh?" he asked.

The tracks snaked down a steep, twisting ravine. On the left was a long, sheer ledge of gray stone hung with snow and ice. On the right, a thick forest of spruce, heavily draped with snow.

The boys stomped out a platform in the snow, packing it down so they'd have a spot to sit and put on their snowboards. They ratcheted down their bindings, zipped up their jackets, and pulled goggles over their eyes. Finally, they pulled on their gloves and stood up.

"Dropping in!" yelled Frogger, kicking his board into the air and hopping off the platform.

Gregory stared, openmouthed. It was as if Frogger were falling down an elevator shaft! The boy flew straight down and disappeared around a corner before Gregory could even blink.

"Watch out for the first couple turns," Tyler said, as he stood up to follow his friend. "It's a little tight in there." He hopped off the platform and zipped out of sight.

Jason adjusted his goggles. "Here goes!" he said, grinning. "Have a blast, man." And he was gone.

Gregory's heart was banging in his chest. He looked back up the trail, the way they had come. Should he just turn and walk out? He'd be back at the gondola station in no time, and he could cruise down one of the mellow, open trails, enjoying a relaxing ride to the bottom.

So what if these guys thought he was chicken? It wasn't as if he'd been riding at North Woods since he was three years old, the way they had. Maybe he needed a little more practice before he could keep up with them.

Or maybe not. They seemed to think he was up to it. Maybe he really *was* being a chicken if he didn't at least *try*. After all, he reasoned, how much trouble could he get into? If worse came to worst, he could take off his snowboard and hike down the hill.

Either way, he had to decide fast. If he had any hope of catching up with his friends, he couldn't delay any longer. Gregory reached down to tighten his bindings. Then he stood up, pulled on his gloves, and took a long, deep breath.

He looked down the trail. His heart thudded. He closed his eyes for a second. Then he opened them and hopped off the platform, down the narrow trail.

"Hey!" yelled the lift attendant. "What the heck?" He turned, outraged, to face his coworker at the loading station for the gondola. "Did you see that?"

"Yeah, it was cool," said the man who had been helping people load their skis into the slots on the outside of a capsule. "That dog just ran right into the gondola. Guess he wants to check out the top of the mountain!"

Santa Paws panted a little as he tried to find a comfortable place to lie down. He'd run as fast as he could when Steve had opened the door of ski patrol headquarters. He wasn't even sure where he was going — until he saw the car-sized metal capsules sliding uphill, attached to a cable that hung high above the open slopes. Without breaking stride, he ran right up to the door of one of the capsules and leapt inside as it moved past.

"Well, hello, there!" said a man in a blue jacket. He was sitting on one of the two benches that faced each other across the gondola car. "Where are your skis, pup?"

The woman sitting next to him laughed. "He looks as if he knows just where he's going," she marveled. "I guess he must ride this gondola all the time." She reached down to scratch his ears.

Santa Paws usually *loved* to have his ears scratched, but right now he had more serious things on his mind. He was practically quivering with determination as he sniffed the air and listened hard for any clues. Somewhere, high on the mountain, Gregory was in trouble. Big trouble. And it was up to Santa Paws to find him.

The snow continued to pack in around Gregory's body. He felt its pressure on his chest and shoulders, and the area around his mouth — the area where there was still oxygen to breathe — was growing smaller every second as his warm breath formed the snow into an icy mask.

How could this have happened?

The last thing he remembered was falling, for what seemed like the fortieth time, face-first into soft snow. All the other times, he'd managed to get up again, although it took more effort every time. Trying to get your legs untangled and stand up in the soft, deep powder was a *lot* of work.

The trail had been rough going. Gregory was soaked with sweat. The sleeve of his jacket had caught on a branch and torn. One of his gloves was wet, and his hand was freezing. And his goggles kept fogging up, which made it even harder to see.

Once he found himself upright again after a fall, he'd stand for a moment, listening. Hoping to hear the familiar hoots and hollers of Tyler, Frogger, and Jason. But they were so far ahead of him. In fact, they were probably all the way at the bottom by then, and on their way to the cafeteria for their usual dinner of cheeseburgers and chili fries. His new friends. Ha! They probably hadn't given him a second thought as they propped their boards on a rack and sauntered into the lodge, checking out the girls and laughing about their wild ride in the Zoo.

So. He was alone in the Zoo. Gregory had decided that his best course of action was simply to get himself down the mountain safely. Nobody had to know that he had not shredded the trail, hitting every turn with style the way Frogger did. He could work his way down slowly and carefully.

Or could he? It seemed that no matter how careful he was, he soon found himself flailing in the deep snow again, sinking up to his hips in what was beginning to feel like quicksand.

Gregory tried hard not to think about that time in New Hampshire, so many years ago. The time when Uncle Steve was hurt so badly, and Gregory and Patricia had to make their way through the winter wilderness for help. That was a time that Gregory had worked to forget. Sometimes he still had nightmares about being lost in a snowy forest, yelling and yelling for help. In the nightmares, he was alone. That time in the Whites, at least he'd had Patricia and Santa Paws for company.

Now, he was alone for real. And he was afraid.

If only he could just take off his board and *walk* out. But that was impossible. The barely tracked snow in the woods was far too soft and deep. It would take hours to work his way down the mountain, and by then it would be completely dark. As it was, he was finding it harder and harder to see which way the twisting trail went as it threaded its way between the spruces.

Should he stop where he was and try to build a shelter? Hole up for the night? Maybe that would be the wisest thing. When they realized he was missing, his family would organize a search party. They'd find him and take him back to the Winterhaus. He'd soak in the hot tub until he was warm all the way through, and then he'd eat a huge dinner and tell the story of his day.

But — would it really happen that way? Or would he freeze to death on this tiny, little-known, illegal trail, where his tracks were covered by falling snow? He was already cold and wet, and he had no food with him at all, not even the sports bar he usually kept in the pocket of his ski pants. He'd wolfed that down hours ago.

Gregory decided he had to keep going. How long could it take to make his way back to the base lodge? Surely he would be there before it was completely dark.

He shoved off again, carefully edging his board to check his speed as much as possible.

And then — the big fall. He would never know what caused it. But this one wasn't like the others. This time, no matter how he tried, he absolutely could not get up. In fact, he could hardly move at all. He was upside down in the snow, helplessly tangled in the branches of a tree. And it was getting harder and harder to breathe.

"Help!" he cried again.

* * *

At the bottom of the gondola, Steve and Mark hurled questions at the lift attendants. "Did you see four boys get on this lift?" Mark asked. "Snowboarders?"

"What about a dog?" Steve asked. "Did you see a dog?"

The liftie held up his hands. "Boarders, sure. Tons of 'em, all day. They're loving this powder. And, yeah, I saw a dog. Wildest thing I ever saw in the ten years I've been working here. He just ran right into one of the gondolas like he'd been doing it every day."

Steve and Mark looked at each other. Then Mark spoke into his radio. "Mark to base," he said. "Begin Search and Rescue procedures."

13

The dog stood quivering as the metal capsule began to slow down, entering the building at the top of the mountain. His nose was against the door, waiting for it to open so he could bolt out and find Gregory's tracks.

"Nice riding with you, pooch," said the man in the blue jacket, as he stood up and pulled on his hat.

"That's one serious dog," said the woman. "He's all business. Wonder what he's so keyed up about?"

Just then, the gondola's door began to slide open. In a heartbeat, Santa Paws had leapt out. He dodged the lift attendant who was standing nearby and took off at a run to the exit from the gondola station.

"Hey!" said the liftie to his partner. "That must be the dog they radioed us about. We're supposed to pay attention to which way he goes."

"I'll follow him." The man pulled on a helmet

127

and ran out after Santa Paws. He hopped onto a snowmobile parked just outside the gondola station, revved the motor, and took off after Santa Paws, who was just disappearing up the hill. "Jake to base," radioed the lift attendant. "The dog is heading for the traverse to the Zoo. I'll follow as far as I can."

Inside their gondola car, Mark and Steve heard Jake's report. Mark nodded. "Just what I figured," he said. "Those kids can't stay out of the woods."

"Is that the same trail we used to call the Jungle?" Steve asked. "I seem to remember taking a few unauthorized trips in there myself."

Mark smiled in spite of himself. "That's right," he said. "I guess I've ducked a few ropes in my time, too." Then he frowned. "But it's no place to head at this time of day. And from what you've told me, your nephew hasn't been boarding long enough or often enough to be on a trail like that."

Steve glanced toward the gondola windows. Snow was still falling, and the light was beginning to wane. "It's getting dark," he said. "I just hope Gregory's okay."

Gregory was beginning to feel faint. He was so wet and cold, so hungry, so very, very tired. All he really wanted to do was fall asleep, forget that any of this was happening. But something deep inside told him that if he did, he might never wake up. "Stay awake!" he ordered himself. He tried one more time to move his arms, to push the ice away from his mouth. But he was more trapped than ever, as the snow packed in around him. He was like a mummy in a casket, unable to move a muscle. Gregory thought of his mother and father and how sad they would be if he died out here, all by himself in the woods. Even Patricia would probably shed a tear or two, if only because she wouldn't have her big little brother, as she called him, to tease anymore. And Santa Paws? The dog would never understand why Gregory had left him. He would feel abandoned all over again, the way he'd been abandoned as a puppy. Gregory couldn't do that to Santa Paws. He just couldn't.

Gathering all of his remaining energy, he shouted out as loudly as he could. "Santa Paws! Help! Help me!"

Far above Gregory, the dog stood stock-still for a moment, his ears pricked and his nose quivering. He had followed the faint trail into the woods and across the mountain until he had come to the place where Gregory and the other boys had sat in the snow. By then, the noisy snowmobile following Santa Paws had been forced, by deep snow and thick forest, to stop. That meant Santa Paws could hear the very, very faint sound coming from down the hill. It was nothing more than a whisper on the wind by the time it reached his ears, but to the dog the sound was unmistakable. It was Gregory. The boy was still alive — but he wouldn't be for long!

The dog could also hear people approaching behind him on the trail, and the crackle of radios. He even heard a voice he recognized as Steve's. But he didn't wait. He leapt off the platform and into the deep, soft snow below. Soon he was careening down the hill, not even trying to slow himself down as he surfed through the snow, ducking around trees as he tried to follow the path made by Gregory's snowboard. There weren't many scent clues, and the few that had been left were rapidly being covered by the falling snow, but Santa Paws did not hesitate or slow down. Here was a place where Gregory had fallen. Here was a spot where Gregory's shoulder had grazed a tree. Santa Paws was so intent on his trail that he paid no attention to his footing. Once he slipped over a small, rocky cliff and dove snout-first into a snowbank that threatened to trap him. But he dug his way out, clawing with his front feet and pushing with his rear legs. And the second he surfaced, he was off again, without even pausing for breath.

Down at patrol headquarters, Mrs. Callahan sat near the radio, wrapped in a blanket but still shivering a bit while Mr. Callahan rubbed her cold hands. Rachel and her new friend, Robert, had pulled up chairs nearby. Emily lay on one of the treatment beds, her ankle splinted and propped up on a pile of pillows, while Patricia lay on the other, still icing her knee. Miranda and Lucy were in the lounge, busily coloring in a tattered Snow White coloring book as they snacked on microwave popcorn. Cookie lay under the table, watching intently for every kernel that fell and grabbing it up instantly, crunching happily each time. Miranda kept her friend busy by dropping nearly as many kernels as she ate.

"Maybe he's just in the cafeteria," Mrs. Callahan said quietly. They had told the younger girls that Gregory was still having too much fun snowboarding and that dinner would be a little late.

Tom shook his head. "That's the first place they look when they start a search," he told her.

"Don't those guys live nearby, the ones he's been hanging out with?" Patricia asked. "Maybe they went to somebody's house."

"They've checked," said Mr. Callahan. "Nobody's sure where those kids are, but they're not home."

"So maybe they're all together?" Eileen asked hopefully.

This time, Maria broke the bad news. "Nope," she said. "The three locals were seen in the cafeteria a half hour ago. But they took off before we could question them."

Just then, the radio crackled. "Mark to base," said a voice.

Maria grabbed the microphone. "This is base, go ahead," she said.

"We've found tracks," Mark reported. "Snow-board tracks and dog tracks. We're following them down."

"What's your twenty?" Maria asked.

"The Zoo," Mark said shortly.

"Roger," said Maria. "Get back to us when you have any news. I'll have a snowmobile ready to go." She turned to Eileen. "Looks as if they're on the trail, anyway," she said. "They'll find him soon."

"What does 'twenty' mean?" Mrs. Callahan asked.

"Location," Patricia told her mother, before Maria could answer. "It's a ten-code. All kinds of emergency workers and police use ten-codes. Like ten-four? That means 'I hear you.' Twenty is short for ten-twenty. Now, if Mark wanted to let us know that there was, say, a crime in progress, he'd say 'ten-thirty-one.' It's like a whole language." Patricia had always loved having a police officer uncle who could teach her all the behind-the-scenes facts. She'd learned her ten-codes before she was eight years old.

Mrs. Callahan nodded, but she wasn't paying

complete attention to Patricia. She stared at the radio as if she could will it to crackle again, with the news that Gregory had been found.

"This is a lot steeper than I remembered!" Steve yelled to Mark. They were working their way on skis down the narrow, twisting trail. It was almost dark now, and both men were wearing headlamps that lit up the path. AJ and Andy followed behind them on snowshoes, carrying a portable litter that could be used for transporting an injured person out of the woods.

"But you still have the moves," Mark called back. "I haven't seen you fall once yet."

"Too scared to fall," Steve said jokingly. But in truth he *was* a little frightened. This whole adventure was bringing back the Christmas of the plane crash. If only he could help Gregory the way the boy had helped him all those years ago. He remembered how frustrating it had been, lying cold and helpless in the makeshift shelter, too injured to move. He'd hated to send his young niece and nephew into the winter wilderness, looking for help. But he'd had no choice. And with the dog's help, they had all survived. Would Santa Paws be able to pull it off again?

Farther down the trail, the dog had begun to lose energy. His muscles were exhausted from working his way through the snow, and it had been hours and hours since he had eaten. There were moments when he lost Gregory's scent entirely and had to backtrack through the drifts, dodging tree branches that threatened to scratch his face. He hadn't heard anything from below for some time now, only the sounds of men following close behind him. He stopped to listen. Then he sniffed the air. Sniffed again. He was close, so close! Why couldn't he hear Gregory calling anymore?

Suddenly, Santa Paws bounded three long steps down the trail. He stuck his nose deep into the snow and sniffed again. Yes! This was it! He was almost there! Two more bounds, and suddenly, through the gathering darkness, he saw something. A leg! Gregory's leg. He pushed his nose between the spiky branches and took a long sniff. Yes! Gregory's leg! Then he began to bark as loud as he could.

"Hear that?" Steve yelled to Mark. "That's Santa Paws! He's found him!" Both men sped up, whipping their skis around turns they could barely make out through the darkness and snow-laden trees.

Santa Paws was digging as hard as he ever had. Only this time, he wasn't going to get yelled at for ruining the garden. He wasn't going to find a bone, either. He was going to find something much, much better. His paws were a blur as he blasted snow behind him into a growing pile. The scent of Gregory grew stronger and stronger as the boy's body was revealed. Finally, Santa Paws slowed down his furious pace as he came closer to Gregory's shoulders and head. Carefully, he scraped away the last of the snow around the boy's mouth.

"Santa Paws!" Steve burst into the small clearing where the dog was working. "Did you find him? Is he all right?"

There was a choking noise, a long intake of breath. "Uncle Steve?" Gregory said weakly. "Santa Paws? Is that you?"

Cheers erupted in ski patrol headquarters when Mark radioed that Gregory had been found.

"And he says Gregory isn't injured at all — no broken bones or even a sprain!" Maria reported, after listening to more. "He was stuck in what's known as a tree well — very dangerous! But they've extricated him, and they're bringing him out onto the main trail. We'll have a snowmobile meet them, and he'll be down here within minutes. Once we get him warmed up, he'll be as good as new."

"I suppose this means we have to let him have the first shower," Patricia said to Rachel. But she hugged her friend hard, and there were tears in her eyes.

14

"More pancakes, Granddad?" Patricia asked, passing the platter to her grandfather. It was Christmas morning at the Winterhaus. The snowstorm had finally petered out in the middle of the night, and the Callahan grandparents had had no trouble driving to the B and B. Rachel's parents had called to say that they were on their way and would be picking her up by noon. And, judging by the stack of presents under the tree, Santa had indeed figured out where the Callahans were staying.

Patricia's grandfather groaned and patted his stomach. "I wish I could, but I can't fit another bite," he answered. "What a feast! It reminds me of the Christmas breakfasts we had when I was a boy. Hotcakes and sausage and all the maple syrup you could pour."

Grammy refused seconds, too.

"I'll take a few more," said Gregory, reaching for the platter.

"What a surprise," Patricia muttered sarcastically. But she smiled at her brother. He had been eating practically nonstop since the night before, when he'd been carried off the mountain, cold and exhausted but unhurt. He had also been really nice about her injury, bringing her ice for her knee and making sure she was comfortable. Her knee was feeling a lot better, and Uncle Steve had said that if the swelling continued to go down, she'd probably be fine. "Don't suppose you'd like another piece of bacon, too?"

"I'll take two," he said. "One for me, one for my buddy." He helped himself to two strips of bacon and slipped one to Santa Paws, who was lying at his feet beneath the table. "Merry Christmas, big guy," said Gregory. "You're the best."

"Don't forget Cookie," Miranda said. "She's a hero, too. She helped find us when we were lost in the woods, and she stayed with us until the ski patrollers came to help."

"That's right," said Emily. Her ankle was feeling a lot better, but she was still icing it and staying off it as much as possible. "I'll never forget her for it, either. She was a real comfort." She broke off a piece of her muffin and handed it to Cookie. "I know it's not a cookie," she said apologetically, "but it's close."

Cookie accepted the gift graciously, nibbling away at it and spitting out the blueberries.

Mr. Callahan rolled his eyes. "I thought we had *rules* in this family about not feeding dogs from the table."

"Rules, schmules," said Mrs. Callahan. "It's Christmas, and these dogs have been saving lives right and left." She leaned down to hand a piece of syrup-drenched pancake to Santa Paws. "If it weren't for Santa Paws and Cookie — " she broke off, wiping her eyes.

Steve nodded. "My buddies want to give both dogs a special citation at their ski patrol banquet this spring," he said. "We'll have to make another trip up here for that."

Santa Paws chose that moment to let out a huge yawn. Everybody cracked up. "Oh, how boring," Gregory translated. "Another citation. I'll add it to my collection."

The dog didn't know why all the people were laughing, but the sound made him happy. He felt peaceful and content, with his stomach full of good food and all his people nearby, safe and sound. He thumped his tail on the floor and gazed up lovingly at Gregory.

The Callahan family spent the next couple of hours opening lots and lots of presents. Presents from husband to wife, father to son, mother to daughter, cousin to cousin . . . the stack seemed to take forever to unwrap. Finally, every gift had been distributed and opened and the floor was littered with wrapping and ribbons. Miranda leaned into her mother with a contented sigh. "I love Christmas," she said.

"Hey, isn't there one more present for Miranda?" Gregory asked Patricia, giving his sister a significant look.

"Oh, right!" said Patricia. "Cookie, can you help me for a minute?" The bouncy black dog followed Patricia down the hall.

Moments later, they reappeared. Miranda looked eagerly at her cousin, but Patricia wasn't carrying a gift.

"Where's my present?" the little girl asked, confused.

Patricia pointed down at Cookie, who was now wearing a red ribbon tied in a huge bow around her neck.

"What?" Miranda asked. "Do you mean — "

Patricia looked at her parents and Gregory, nodded, and took a deep breath. "Miranda, we've all decided that Cookie and you belong together. She'll always be Santa Paws's best friend, and we'll always love her — but she's your dog from now on."

"Really?" Miranda asked. Her eyes were shining. She whirled around to face her mother. "Is it okay? Can Cookie come to live with us?"

"You bet," said Emily, wiping away a tear.

Steve nodded. "She's part of the family," he said.

Miranda threw her arms around Cookie and

squeezed her. Then she jumped up to hug Patricia, Gregory, and her aunt and uncle. "Thank you, thank you, thank you!" she cried. "Cookie is the best present ever!"

Cookie wasn't sure exactly what was going on, but she could tell that Miranda was happy, and that made *her* happy, so happy that she had to jump up and do some spins and twirls — which made everybody laugh and clap their hands. When they clapped, she took a bow, and they clapped even harder.

"Yay, Cookie!" cheered Miranda.

"You go, girl!" yelled Patricia.

"Show-off," muttered Gregory, but he was smiling, too. You couldn't help but smile when Cookie went into her act.

Lucy had been watching everything with big eyes and a big smile. Now she suddenly spoke up. "Mommy," she said. "Open present!"

"Yeah! Open it!" Miranda joined in. Both girls were dying to know what was in the big white box, so gigantic that it didn't even fit under the Christmas tree.

Steve smiled at his wife. "It's from me," he said. "To remember this Christmas by." He went over to get the box and delivered it to where she was sitting. Emily untied the ribbon, ripped open the paper, and opened the flaps on the big cardboard carton. She reached in and pulled out — a huge, plush toy moose!

"Aaahhh!" Mrs. Callahan cried, recoiling in mock fear. "The dreaded moose!"

Cookie and Santa Paws both stood up and started barking in unison.

Emily laughed until tears came to her eyes, and so did everyone else. "It's perfect," said Emily.

"This whole *Christmas* is pretty perfect," said Mrs. Callahan, looking around at her family. "In fact, despite everything that happened, I think it's the best Christmas ever."